Splinter Universe Presents:
Might-have-beens and First Thoughts
from the Liaden Universe®
Sharon Lee and Steve Miller

COPYRIGHT PAGE

Splinter Universe Presents!
Might-have-beens and First Thoughts
from the Liaden Universe®
Pinbeam Books: www.pinbeambooks.com

All of the content collected in this book has previously been posted to Splinter Universe (www.splinteruniverse.com), with the exception of The Authors' Introduction, which is original to this volume.

Cover design by RL Slather

ISBN: 978-1-948465-10-6

Table of Contents

The Authors' Introduction

As you may or may not know, Bob, back in the early 2000s, Sharon Lee and Steve Miller began hosting a site called Splinter Universe.

The conceit behind Splinter Universe was that it would be a place for Lee and Miller, and Lee, and Miller, to post fun bits that the writing process had made unnecessary to a larger work, or character sketches, or discovery stories–incomplete bits of things, for the most part, or, if you will–Splinters.

Each Splinter was accompanied by author commentary talking about the piece, its strengths, weaknesses, its place in the process of writing, and often lending a bit of history to the piece itself or to the Liaden Universe® as a whole. In short, Splinter Universe was created for the amusement of the authors, and those readers who are amused by such things.

Occasionally, the site would host stories by Guest Authors; or a story from one or both of us, before that story was folded into a chapbook.

On those various terms, Splinter Universe has been a success, though it goes through times of greater and lesser activity.

Given the length of time Splinter Universe has been about its various businesses, it became–somewhat crowded. In fact, it was time–past time, frankly–for a thorough housecleaning. Which Sharon proposed to do.

However–people become fond of things, and the fans of Splinter Universe are no exception. They were concerned–in some cases, *very* concerned–that the material which was to be removed from the website would be lost, *forever*.

We promised that this would not be the case; that the content would be preserved and made available to those who wished to have it.

This book is the proof of that promise.

In the following pages, you will find everything that was taken down from Splinter Universe in April of 2020, in order to tidy things up, and to make room for a proposed large project.

Enjoy–and thank you all.

Sharon Lee and Steve Miller

April 13, 2020

Strings, Strands, and Vines in Motion

On Vantegra

Pleny was worried.

Nothing unusual there–Pleny always worried. Which he would have to be a good thing, Cantra being as heedless as a moth. Whatever, Cantra thought, walking behind like a well-trained 'prentice ought, a moth might be.

The port access way was empty, excepting free-trader Pleny and his soft-walking 'prentice. Given the weather, that was hardly surprising, Cantra thought, pushing her hands deeper into the pockets of her slicker. Ship's overalls would have been warmer, but Pleny had insisted on planet-dress, and had braided an orange ribbon into Cantra's limp, no-color hair with his own hands.

Had she not known better, she would have been warmed by this evidence of brotherly esteem–for only the most desperate *sombi* would snatch a bonded, all-by-the-legal 'prentice. Since she knew her worth to Pleny down to the last shaved quint, his care only put her on alert.

Up ahead, a webwork of sickly green lines intersected the walkway. When they broke through that barrier of light, the port–and the dubious protection of port law–would be behind them. In the city, two freetraders, shivering and obvious in their out-of-current clothing, would be prey to every law-giver and upstanding citizen as wished to make them a gift of trouble.

4

Cantra felt her stomach clench, and she deliberately kept her hands and her thoughts from the weapon that rode at the small of her back. Extraplanetaries were specifically forbidden from carrying weapons among the peaceful and law-abiding world dwellers.

Two steps in front of her, just on the port-side of the guard lights, Pleny checked. Cantra stopped, wondering if this were an abrupt return to sense or –

Her brother, so-called, turned his head and glared at her over his shoulder.

"Stay close, stay quiet, and stay out of trouble," he snapped.

Standard orders—said once already, before they left the ship. It was a measure of the depth of Pleny's worry that he repeated himself now. And a measure of hers that she dared to ask a question regarding this folly.

"What do we want in 'tegra-city, brother?"

She hadn't expected an answer, and she wasn't disappointed. With one more snarl, Pleny squared his shoulders and marched forward. The webwork of light reformed, sheathing his long form in flaring green. The image froze, then flowed as the light-motes reported his bio-print to the port census brain.

Cantra took a deep breath, pulled her fists out of her pockets and followed him.

She closed her eyes in the instant before she hit the web—nothing but plain and fancy cowardice—and gagged as the strands congealed around her, freezing her in place, tightening—and releasing her to her interrupted stride, just barely ahead of panic.

Opening her eyes, she spied Pleny already at the busy cross-street, and stretched her long legs to catch him. Much as she might object to her brother's company under usual conditions, the fact was that there was only one key for *Flicker*, and it hung about Pleny's neck.

That he would leave her dirtside if it came to suit him, she had no doubt whatsoever. He'd left Amril, hadn't he? After he'd picked her pocket for the key.

That they happened to be on a *frakith* world—well, and maybe he'd cut her throat for her, first, rather than risk the chance of her being acquired by a *sombi*-master with a scholarly bent.

She reached Pleny's side as he raised an arm over his head. Three lanes out and two down in the rushing traffic, a tiny public carrier—nothing more than a lifter, a brain, and two open-to-atmosphere benches—ducked, dodged and angled toward them at a speed Cantra considered nothing less than suicidal. The cab being machine-mind, perhaps that aspect didn't concern it.

Pleny grabbed her wrist, not gentle, and hissed, "I said *stay close!*"

"I'm close!" she snarled, and was saved saying the rest of what boiled on the end of her tongue by the arrival of the cab.

"Service?" it asked in a high-pitched, childish voice.

Pleny pushed her; she stumbled, recovered and scrambled into the high rear seat, taking hold of the hand-grips with a will. Had there been straps, she'd have used them, gratefully, but *frakith* didn't care about such comforts. Pleny took his place on the larger bench just behind the brain-box and muttered a destination. The cab emitted a series of barks, spun in place three-sixty, and skated across three parallel and four lateral lanes of traffic.

Cantra closed her eyes.

THE CAB SLOWED, LOSING altitude gently. Cantra smelled brine and wet-rot on the breeze against her face, and cautiously opened her eyes.

The street was narrow, with only two lanes, running sedately side-by-side. Below, the tiered walks were as scant of traffic as the skyways; in the distance, just beyond the flat-roofed buildings, she could see the uneasy gray surface of a sea.

Frowning, she blinked up the map of Vantegra City she'd downloaded from the port tourist brain.

A green mote of light flickered in the map–her present location – and the legend, "Shandlir Street, Vantegra Seaport." As the ship flew, they were hard by the port–the spaceport – though the tangle of streets was nothing she would have wanted to attempt on foot, map or no map.

The cab floated past the first walk, and executed a sharp right turn. Despite her hold on the grips, Cantra gasped, feeling her weight shift dangerously–and then they were level again, hovering next to the blue surface of a private landing dock. A door sighed open.

"Destination achieved," the cab piped. "Please exit at the right."

There was a heartbeat of hesitation before Pleny moved–sliding across his seat rather than risk overbalancing the tiny craft, Cantra saw, and felt a spurt of rare sympathy for her elder sibling.

He got himself out without mishap, and it was her turn. She took a breath, moved, felt the cab ship-steady beneath her boots, and stepped onto the dock. Behind her, she heard the snap of a hatch sealing, spun–the cab was rising, twirling on its axis as it did, heading back to the high traffic lanes and its next fare.

"Come on!" Pleny snapped; she heard the grit of his boot soles against the dock, sighed and turned about, the obedient–the *quiet* and so-respectful–'prentice, following her master down the short blue dock toward a blank blue wall.

It being a *frakith* dock, there were no such things as guardrails, and Cantra kept her eyes scrupulously away from the near, thin edges where ramp met atmosphere. It wasn't that she had no head for heights. 'mong shipborn, she was known for her ability to tolerate height, gravity, noise, and all the other uneasy variables attendant to worldwalking. Not that she was precisely shipborn, no more than Pleny, who seemed to have taken to the life like he'd never spent his first dozen years down-space, as ship cant had it.

The blank blue wall was closer; another three strides and Pleny would run his long nose right through–

Light flared—a crimson lattice-work of light, forming a gate between Pleny and the wall. Cantra twitched toward a stop, but her brother never broke stride. The lattice received him, enveloped him–and let him go. Cantra saw him stagger, a little, before she, too, entered the light's sticky embrace.

Contact, freeze, release. She forced herself to walk on as if there had been no interruption, keeping her sigh behind her teeth. Up ahead, her brother strode on, through the door that hadn't been visible a heartbeat before.

She felt the skin between her shoulder blades tighten, but she kept the pace, and followed him inside.

The hall was narrow and straight, the floor a continuation of the docking stone, bright with the colorless illumination from a dozen wall-mounted glow-panels. At the end of the hall was a man, dressed in an orange unisuit, the hood thrown back to reveal a haughty, narrow face with a shock of space-black hair above it.

"Captain Torvin?" he asked, voice prim and over-precise.

"That's me," Pleny said, which was more-or-less true, allowing for the wide difference in custom between the Rim and the *frakith* worlds. He stopped and tucked his hands into his belt, nonchalance embodied.

"And that?" The doorkeeper stabbed his pointy chin at Cantra. She kept her eyes down, like a decent 'prentice would, and let the master deal.

"My 'prentice."

There was a heartbeat of hesitation. The haughty doorman hadn't been told to expect a 'prentice, Cantra thought, her gut going cold. Pleny had counted on custom–the social convention that said an apprentice was only her master's shadow, ignored in trade and at table, to pass her through at his back. His insurance against the deal going bad, invisible, and the illegal hideaway tucked in her belt...

The man went back a step, clearing the doorway, and bowed slightly, sweeping his hand out in a ritualized gesture of welcome.

"Please, enter. *Bentaji* Zolibrith expects you."

Pleny bowed, short and sharp, and swung through the door, a bit of swagger in his walk, now that there was a high-caste *frakith* at hand to impress.

Soft-foot and smooth, Cantra went after him, eyes down, face neutral. She passed the doorman, hoping that he wasn't augmented in anything but the usual ways. A 'prentice might be excused an accelerated heartbeat and slightly quickened breath on her first visit to so substantial a person as a guildlord. If the doorman were properly deferential, himself, he would only read those indicators as awe. If, on the other hand–

She was through. Biting her lip, she moved, silent now, and careful of her balance on the field. The floor was, to her eye, handpainted porcelain, so fragile that the weight of a mouse might shatter it. The repeller field between the priceless artwork and her destructive bootheels was less than the width of one of that mouse's whiskers—and strong enough to bear <u>Flicker</u>, all six pods attached.

"Captain Torvin. How very good of you to come to me." This voice was rich, smooth—as expensive as the floor. Cantra dared a quick glance up through her lashes, but all she saw was her brother's back, and a long wall of scrolls, neatly rolled and slotted.

"*Bentaji* Zolibrith." Pleny's bow was deep, which Cantra wholeheartedly approved. It was impossible to do too much reverence to the individual who held dominion over such a room. "I am at your service, sir."

For a price, Cantra thought, flicking covert glances about the room. Impossible to tally the treasure that lay in plain sight. She began to have some hope that whatever scheme Pleny had might earn them more cash than trouble.

"Certainly, certainly," the rich voice answered. "But, come, sit with me and let us discuss our business over a glass of wine, like civilized men."

Well, that was going a stretch, Cantra thought, at least on Pleny's behalf. The rich-voiced guildlord, now—but no. A civilized man would not need the services of an edge-trader like Pleny so-called Torvin.

Nonetheless, Pleny agreed to the chair and the glass, for which she couldn't blame him, and followed the host down the room, Cantra, his faithful shadow.

The chairs were set in a corner where two scroll shelves joined. *Frakith* chairs, spun from a substance that glittered like glass and very possibly was just that, with wide, translucent arms.

The host paused by the first chair, forcing Pleny to take the inner, and to Cantra's mind, less favored seat. She followed her brother, eyes modestly down, edge-vision gaining a quick impression of richly worked robes and the sharp shine of jewels. Pleny reached his place, turned and bowed—all polite and civilized, Cantra thought, slipping into the scant space between the chair and the shelf.

"Please, Captain Torvin, sit," the guildlord murmured. Perforce, Pleny sat— carefully, as if the spun glass chair might collapse under his weight. Across from him, *Bentaji* Zolibrith sank lightly into his seat, and disposed his robes gracefully.

From her post behind Pleny, Cantra could now study their host more or less at leisure. He was a small man, his pale hair neatly braided with what she supposed must be the medallions of his rank. His hands were gloved in golden mesh; the fancy work on his robe showed gleams of the same material – intellistrands. Cantra glanced up the length of the shelf beside her, caught a gleam of gold, high up, and felt her stomach tighten once more.

The guildlord and the guildlord's room were. . .in communion, through the interface of the strands. So long as the gloves covering his hands, the threads woven into his robes of office, reported a biologic system in harmony, all would be well. Let the strands report an upset in the balance of the lord's emotions, or his physiology—and the room would act to cleanse itself of threat.

Frakith were fond of such toys. If a device could be made to do a thing—if man could conceive the need of a device which might perform such-and-so a function—depend upon it that the *frakith* had already built the thing and were employing it for some dire or trivial purpose.

The guildlord smoothed his robes once more, raised his face and smiled. It was a narrow face, not unpleasing, though younger than she had—

The thought died. The muscles of the young face took the smile easily. But the eyes—blue and set somewhat close together—the eyes were ancient, calculating and cold.

Cantra felt her blood freeze.

"Honor me," *Bentaji* Zolibrith said in his rich, trained voice, "by sampling a glass of the guild's finest." One golden-gloved hand rose, fingers moving in a small series of subtle gestures. From the larger room came a sound, as of air escaping a hose. A shadow moved, and Pleny turned his head, tracking the motion. The guildlord, Cantra saw, keeping her eyes on the clearer danger, let the smile go, his face settling into lines as austere and as giving as crystal.

Once upon a time, someone had wished for there to be a way to live forever. As bad luck would have it, the wish was said within hearing of a *frakith*, who immediately put his thought on how to produce a device to accomplish it. And, *frakith* being *frakith*, they had accomplished it, after a fashion only *frakith* would find acceptable.

Cantra's peculiar and particular studies had included information regarding this device, which was nothing more than a thin golden circlet, which was settled on the brow. The circlet was in communion with a storage tile, to which it downloaded all of the past experiences, memories, emotion—the entire *self*—of a certain person. Most usually this procedure was performed as that certain person lay dying, though that point was moot, as the total eradication of the self induced fatal trauma.

The next person to don the circlet, then, accepted the download of the stored self, allowing it to live on. Some *frakith* liked this scheme so well that they uploaded and downloaded themselves serially, achieving, yes, immortality.

For some definition of immortality.

Guildlord Zolibrith was one such. The eyes told the tale. Cantra could not hazard a guess as to precisely how old he might be, but she would wager atmosphere to vacuum that this was not his first life. Nor even his third.

The soft whisper of escaping air claimed her attention. She glanced away from those too-old eyes with something very like relief and looked to the entrance to the alcove, where came a spun-glass table bearing two fluted glasses filled with ruby liquid. The table progressed steadily, at a height of about Cantra's waist above the floor, and paused by the guildlord's chair. He lifted a glass in a golden hand. The table drifted to Pleny, who received the remaining glass with really commendable nonchalance.

Bentaji Zolibrith raised his glass, tipping it slightly toward Pleny.

"Please, honor me with your opinion."

Pleny sipped—doing justice to the wine and reasonable caution, both—and sat a moment in consideration.

"A subtle vintage," he said at last, and it was genuine respect in his voice, immediately recognizable, though seldom enough heard. He sipped again, and the guildmaster smiled, before lifting his glass to his lips.

Pleny shifted slightly in his chair, and put the glass on the wide chair arm.

"I hope I do not offend," he said, carefully, "if I introduce the subject of business. I had received the impression from Fraumin Belgase that there was some. . .urgency to the matter."

"Urgency. . ." The guildlord tasted the word, languidly, swirling his wine gently in the glass. "Yes, I suppose one might say there is some urgency to the matter, now that events are in motion." He sipped wine and the muscles of his face smiled once more.

"The package is ready," he said softly. "When we are done our wine, you will be escorted to the garage, where you will find a lorry waiting to bear you back to your ship. Once you have offloaded that which you will find in the cargo compartment, the lorry will. . .execute its second level of programming."

Pleny inclined his head. "I understand," he murmured, all polite and high-caste. He moved a hand, aping the guildlord's graceful gesture.

"Fraumin Belgase had named a sum. . .?"

"Certainly, certainly! Have no anxiety, sir; payment will be made before we two part."

Cantra blinked. *That* was something exceptional, payment more usually coming in halves – the up-front to push and the back-end to pull. The guildlord was no fool, after all; he must have thought that edge-traders are risky folk. He had *hired* them because they were risky folk and he had risky business to do.

"Thank you, sir," Pleny said, even more polite. The guildlord moved a glittering hand.

"Common practice, I assure you," he said, airily. The cold, old eyes sharpened.

"But, come, Captain Torvin, you are not drinking! Do you find my little vintage unworthy, after all?"

Cantra took a breath. It was an article of faith with them–all of them–never to drink all the wine, or consume all the food that was offered, down-space. *Why overworkthe system?* Amril had used to say.

Still, there were times when the drink could not be spilled, or the food slipped into a pocket. It would never do to offend the guildlord while they were still owed what Cantra very much hoped was a tidy sum in hard currency.

Pleny's calculations had taken less time than hers; the glass was already in his hand.

"Truly, sir, I wished to have a plain business understanding between us so that I might savor the reminder of this vintage in harmony with yourself."

A pretty speech, Cantra allowed, if entirely untrue.

The guildlord raised his glass with a grand flourish. "Well, then–a toast to the success of our joint enterprise!"

Pleny's flourish was considerably less grand. "To success!" he repeated and sipped.

"A pity you do not have time to visit the vineyard which produces this vintage," *Bentaji* Zolibrith said softly, his glass held loosely between golden fingers. "The mother of our vines is surely the most accomplished of all those now nurturing, the product of a line unbroken over six dozen generations."

Cantra considered that, wondering if the purity of the master vintner's line had been preserved by *frakith* tech, and, if so, what form that tech might take. She was still worrying at that puzzle when Pleny set his glass down.

"So," said the guildlord, rising at once, in a smooth, effortless flow, "to business!"

THE LIFT WAS ENCLOSED, for a *frakith* wonder; the only indication of their speed or direction a row of red pinlights, which lit, one after the other, following the same route from ceiling edge to floor, over and over again. Cantra stood at the back of the compartment, Pleny and the unisuited security before her, all facing the door–or, at least, the wall that had been the door when they entered–and silent.

Pleny, Cantra thought, was likely congratulating himself on his success so far. And, to be just, that success was not inconsiderable, measured in hard coin, as it had been. The *frakith* chest containing that coin sat on the floor between Cantra's feet. All that remained was to do the job.

Whatever it was.

The pinlight line snapped to a solid bar of red, blinked twice and went out. The wall they were all facing slid silently away, revealing a steel-walled bay, the promised lorry standing hard by.

Security exited first, followed by Pleny, followed by Cantra, box on shoulder.

The door to the passenger compartment stood open. Pleny paused.

"Our package?" he asked the security man.

"Loaded and locked," the other replied.

Pleny frowned, and Cantra could follow the line of his thought as if it were her own.

Here's a man pays good–very good–money to have a certain package up-space and away. So he says. What odds the deal is a different deal, with two edge-traders set up and sacrificed, the cash recovered later? What odds, if those dice didn't roll a winner, that the security man, here, was up for a little bait-and-switch? Or, hold–what odds that–

"I'll see that the package is in place," Pleny said. "Captain's Prerogative."

Security didn't like it, but he didn't argue it, either. Might have been he'd done some space. Might have been he'd studied, much as Cantra had.

Shrugging, he went 'round to the back, twisted the catch and shoved the gate up.

The package was locked into the first bay–a low steel box about as long as Cantra was tall, and a half-a-dozen hands wide, sealed with nothing more exotic than ordinary cargo-cord.

So, the package was in place. Captain's Prerogative did stretch to unsealing the box and inspecting the contents, and Cantra saw Pleny take an extra breath or so to consider it. In the end, he came down on the side of not irritating Security unduly, which was a reasonable decision, if not precisely the one Cantra thought she would have made.

He stepped back, caught her eye and jerked his head. She, obedient 'prentice, went forward, swung the treasure-box down from her shoulder and slid it into the bay behind the package. There came a sturdy *snap* as the lock-downs took hold, Cantra ducked back and Security slammed the gate.

Pleny walked back 'round to the front of the lorry, Cantra after, Security following both. She hoisted herself up and onto the back bench. No belts, of course, but she tried to take comfort from the fact that the compartment was enclosed.

"Just give the navigator the coordinates of your ship," Security said, as Pleny climbed into the front and settled himself around the smooth dome that housed the lorry's brain.

"What about sending it home?" he asked

"Pre-programmed," said Security, and touched the side of the compartment, ducking away from the descending door. It locked with a boom, leaving them enclosed, with what illumination came from the faintly glowing floor.

"No screen?" Cantra dared ask, when she had counted three heartbeats and Pleny had not bespoken the navigator.

He sighed, very softly, and she resigned herself to receiving no reply.

But—"Apparently not," said her brother, and leaned to whisper *Flicker's* direction to the lorry's brain.

SHE'D NOT HAVE CREDITED the assertion that there was any more harrowing travel than open to the wind on a *frakith* cab, or that the lorry's blind, frictionless crawl could have so quickly eroded her equilibrium. By the time the door swung up and away, revealing *Flicker's* own cargo-lift before them, Cantra had twice regulated her breathing and her pulse, and was considering the wisdom of going to a secondary state for the duration.

To judge by her brother's rapid exit of the pilot's bench, he had suffered a similar crisis of function.

"Quickly!" he hissed at her and she slid out of the compartment and round to the back, where he had the gate up.

Cantra pulled a key out of her belt, and slapped it against bay one's lock. The affect of the field unlocking was so strong that the treasure-box bounced a little, and the payload swung, cargo-cord grating against the smart-tile floor.

"Get the pallet jack," Pleny directed, swinging up into the bay. He jerked his head at the smaller box. "Send that up the chute."

"Aye," she said, and ran to do both.

The package was heavier even than Cantra had judged, and it took both of them and the jack in overdrive to get it offloaded and onto the lift. Cantra looked back at the lorry, in the instant before the door sealed, and saw a shimmer 'round the body, as if it were hot, and giving off its heat in waves–

And then the door came closed and they were rising, back to the safety of their ship.

BETWEEN THEM, THEY wrestled the package off the lift and into the first of the interior holds. They got it off the jack and locked; Cantra reached for the cord–

"Get the jack stowed," Pleny said sharply, grabbing her wrist. "Then file us a lift with admin."

Her temper flared, and she wrenched free.

"File us a lift to *where*?" she snarled. "What d'you take as a reasonable percentage, in fast money?"

Pleny glared at her. "File us for Kineo, why not, little sister? Just a standard lift-out, is all, when the pattern favors us. No reason to call attention to ourselves. Is there, Cantra?"

She was breathing too hard. She took care of that, then held out her hand.

"Give over the key, then."

He jerked the chain over his head and threw it at her, the links whipping nastily toward her face. She flung an arm out and the chain wrapped snuggly around her sleeve.

"Lift out, no hurry," she said, by way of verifying her orders. "Filed for Kineo."

Pleny grunted, which she took for yes, his eyes already hard on the package. Cantra shrugged, cycled the jack and steered it out of the hold.

THE PATTERN GAVE THEM a clean lift within a double *kwatrane.* Cantra verified the numbers with admin's brain and locked the course, then hit the supplies inventory. They were down on non-synth foodables, the synthetic being nourishment of last resort with Pleny. Cantra never minded what she was eating, a function she usually performed with both eyes on a scroll. Pleny, though, craved cheeses, soft breads, beers, and sweet fruits.

Flicking through the port directory, she found a green-grocer that would supply those things, quicktime, at only a twelve percent markup, and placed the order, giving berth number and cargo-lift orientation. She transferred the funds from ship's account to the grocer's, with a hold on release until delivery was taken.

That done, she upped the mag on the screen that monitored the cargo-lift–and, frowning, upped it again.

Directly before the lift, obvious against the pale blast surface, was a pile of grey matter–dust, she thought, increasing the magnification a third time. But would dust scramble and crumple in on itself, or–she slapped the heat sensor on, and coded the mag to the top.

The sensor found a little heat in the rapidly moving dust pile, a reading that dropped even as she watched it. The dust pile itself–was not dust, but countless tiny machines, growing steadily less as the more mobile turned upon and devoured their lesser brethren.

Fingers flying, Cantra accessed the cargo eye, rolled the recording back to the top of the hour and watched as she and Pleny wrestled the pallet jack and the package onto the lift, catching a glimpse of her own wary face just before the door closed and the lorry began to melt.

It went quickly, eroding into dust which the tiny machines devoured before turning upon and devouring themselves. The record ran into real-time, showing her the clean, pale surface–and then another lorry, painted bright green, with the grocer's glyph large on the side pulled up, gate lifting.

Still frowning, Cantra stood, jerked the key from its slot on the board, and went down to the lift, dropping the chain over her head as she went.

SOME WHILE LATER, FOODABLES stowed and the time coming worrisome close to lift, she went in search of her brother.

He wasn't in quarters, nor yet in bio. No reason for him to be in the library, but she checked anyway, finding the chamber locked and dark.

Frowning, Cantra checked the time. She could lift *Flicker*, if it came to it–the ship's key hung for a change 'round *her* neck. Problem was, she'd caught some of the glances Pleny was starting to throw her way. Soon now, it wasn't going to matter that she was his insurance in strange ports and his back-up on ship. Soon, Pleny was going to convince himself that she was a deadly danger to him–just like he'd done with Amril. Amril, who had been the keenest and the kindest of them all, without who none of them would have gotten out of the–

She moved her head, shaking away bad memories, and stretched her legs, heading for cargo. That Pleny would ultimately betray her was inevitable, and something she neither could nor wished to prevent. But she could damn well make sure that he abandoned her someplace where she had a credible chance of surviving long enough to find another ship. Which particular paradise did not include anywhere so *frakith* as Vantegra. Best then not to excite paranoia by reminding her brother that she could pilot *Flicker* as well as he could.

A shadow moved at the joining of the main hall with cargo, and there was the missing, not quite running, face slightly damp. His eye fell on her and he snarled.

"Get to the tower! Don't we have lift?"

Cantra reversed direction smoothly and headed back the way she'd come, keeping two steps ahead of him.

"Came looking for the pilot," she said, forcibly calm. "So lift could go forward."

Behind her, she heard labored breathing, and dared a glance over a shoulder.

Pleny was a long-nosed, sharp-faced, unhandsome fellow, and his sister Cantra was another just like him. That given, he'd rarely looked so poorly as he did right then, with the sweat sheeting his face and dripping off the end of his nose.

"What's amiss?" she demanded and earned another snarl for her sisterly solicitude.

"Nothing! Give me the key!"

She pulled the chain over her head with alacrity, and swung aside, back to the corridor wall, the key swinging from her outstretched hand.

He snatched it away and lumbered by, running for some definition of the act, but with none of the surefooted grace bred into them all.

The wine, she thought, stomach clenching, and hurried after him, down the long corridor and up the stairs to the piloting chamber.

THEY LIFTED FOR KINEO, right enough, and as soon as the alignments favored them, altered course for a lesser-known translation point on the risky side of the equations. Cantra ran the co-pilot's share–communication, scan, shields–and kept herself as close to invisible as possible.

Pleny leaned over the pilot's side like a man who had taken his death, crumpled at the waist and canted to the right. The straps held him up, and his hands moved with precision. But his face was gray now–almost a match for the metal hull, and his down-space silks were soaked with sweat.

His hands moved once more, locking the amended course into *Flicker's* navigation brain–and again, to unlock his straps.

Leaning hard on the arms of the pilot's chair, he pushed himself to his feet and stared down at her out of glazed brown eyes.

"I'm going to quarters," he said, thickly. "Keep the course."

"Aye," Cantra said, without inflection.

Whether Pleny heard her, she didn't know. He turned and staggered away, one hand hard against the wall.

TRANSLATION WAS SOME while in the past, drop-out some while still in the future. In the boredom between, Cantra fed herself, showered, napped, and came back to the tower, excepting to find Pleny at the board before her.

The tower was empty, the go-lights showing stable, ship's key an iridescent glow in its nesting place at the center of the board.

Biting her lip, Cantra stepped forward, hesitated at the pilot's station and went past it to the co-pilot's couch. She fed in her code and accessed the navigator, running a re-calc in her head more as a calming exercise than in expectation of finding serious trouble to shoot. There was a little drift in the numbers, *Flicker's* navigator being slightly idiot, and she fed in the corrections, no more than half attending what she did.

Corrections accepted and locked, she sat a moment, then bent forward fast, not giving herself a chance to argue the con side, snapped on an open line in-ship and cleared her throat.

"Pleny, respond to tower," she said, her voice sounding tense in her own ears, her brother's gray and sweating face all too vivid before the eyes of memory. "Pleny, we re-enter normal space in one *kwatrane*." She paused to struggle briefly with herself before adding. "Brother, if you are in need of aid, only call, and I will come."

She sat back, then, sensors set on the broadest band possible, and listened.

For a while, there was nothing to hear save the rub of air against the equipment, which, Cantra thought, she might take as either a hopeful sign on a dire one. She and her sibs were tough and resilient. If the *frakith* wine had gotten the better of Pleny for a little time, the odds were very, very good that in the end her brother would have prevailed. The cost of such victories was sometimes counted in many *kwatranes* of deep sleep, from which he would certainly not rouse simply to reassure his favorite sister, Cantra.

She leaned forward, hand outstretched to cancel the scan and–a sound issued from the pick-up.

A groan, deep and breathless, traced to the interior hold where they had stashed the *frakith* cargo. Cantra thought a curse–did not give it voice.

The groan came again, slightly louder, and sounding not at all like Pleny Torvin.

Cantra locked her board as she surged to her feet, running out of the tower and down to cargo.

THE HOLD WAS EMPTY, save the package–cargo cord undone, top ajar. Of Pleny, there was no sign.

Amril had used to say that Torvinlab had, on one slow day, spun cat-strands into those they'd been refining, and that half-serious experiment had yielded Cantra. Certainly, she had more active curiosity than the rest of her sibs, totaled, which was why they'd set her to study and cipher.

Quickly, she stepped to the side of the open package, expecting to see nothing, but unable to deny herself a look.

Her curiosity was rewarded, for what she glimpsed under the gaping lid was not merely the empty metallic gleam of the interior, but–a face, a form, and, as she leaned closer–a groan, breathless and deep.

Cantra grabbed the lid and shoved it aside to totter for a moment, and then clang noisily to the floor. A breath of warm air struck her face, tasting faintly of wine. The woman in the sarcophagus muttered, her wild brows pulling together; long brown fingers plucking fretfully at her diaphanous wrap.

Gripping the edges of the box, Cantra stared. Warm goods. She took a breath, deliberately bringing her rage and her horror down into dispassion.

Pleny agreed to ship warm goods, she thought, and horror spiked again, despite her best efforts.

The *fool*.

The woman in the box muttered, muted liquid sounds from no language that Cantra knew. She focused her attention, noting that this woman had been radically augmented, as often purchased courtesans were, to more greatly pleasure their owners. Though what pleasure one might find in hair of tangled leaf and twig, fingers gnarled like long roots, and a sharp boned face all covered in pale green down, strayed beyond Cantra's understanding.

She shuddered where she stood, bent over the unconscious captive. Augmentation was surely not strange to her, with the past she had behind her. And yet–she shivered again, and put dangerous thoughts away, and looked once more to the other.

Her ears were tiny and close to her head; the lobe of the right one was torn, as if an ornament had been yanked free, with no regard for the damage done.

And why, after all, Cantra thought, recalling the guildlord in his robes, and his subtle, gold-meshed hands–why should there have been any care taken of one who had displeased the master?

And why, she asked herself, then, would one who had displeased the master not simply be relieved of her life?

What had Pleny agreed to, for that *frakith* chest full of coin?

She closed her eyes. Perhaps the woman in the casket had been sold? she thought hopefully. And Pleny Torvin had agreed to do nothing other than escort her to her new owner?

It was a comforting thought, and she rejected it immediately. Pleny's fee had been too large to purchase any lawful service.

"*Sanatharu evaji?*" The voice was light and sweet.

Cantra opened her eyes. The woman in the casket was twisting, fingers pulling at the wraps as if they constricted her.

"Evaji?" she said again, writhing, her voice rising toward panic. "*Evaji te andal! Te andal!*"

Cantra reached down, gripped the frail covering where it lay against the inner wall of the casket and pulled. There was a moment of strong resistence before the cloth came free, revealing a corded brown body loosely clad in a short white shift; her feet, as long and gnarly as her hands, were bare. Cantra yanked the restraint from its anchorage on the second wall and flung it to the floor.

In the casket, the captive stilled, took a hard, deliberate breath—and opened her eyes.

Red they were, deeply so, very much of a color with the guildlord's wine, with no white to be seen, and the long dark lashes curling up. She stared into Cantra's face, her sharp, downy features tightening.

Cantra raised her hands, fingers spread, in the common sign for *peace*. The woman took another deliberate breath, and raised both of her long, gnarly appendages, in imitation.

"Where," she said, halting, as if her tongue were not quite accustomed to the taste of the mercantile language, "do I awake? In the care of friend? Or foe?"

Well, now, that *was* the question wasn't it? Cantra thought.

Slowly, displaying no threat, she lowered her hands to her sides.

"You find yourself a passenger on the good ship *Flicker*," she said, taking care to speak each word clearly, in consideration of an unpracticed ear. "I am Cantra, 'prentice to Captain-Owner Pleny Torvin."

"Ship," the other repeated. "To what shore are we then bound?"

Another pointed question, that. Cantra sighed. "Kineo," she said, that being last filed, and no need for this woman, just yet, to know more than Vantegra Port.

The wild brows pulled together and the ruby eyes narrowed.

"That is no port known to me or to my house," the woman in the box said at last. "I think that this must be no proper seaship."

"Seaship, no," said Cantra. "*Flicker* sails the stars."

The ruby eyes flew wide. "The stars," she repeated, toneless.

"Just so," Cantra assured her briskly. "Now, you have had courtesy of me—my name, the name of my captain, my ship and the port to which we are bound. May I not have your name?"

The deep red eyes gazed up into her face, expressionless. An old game. Cantra returned stare for stare, her breathing slow and sure. The woman in the casket looked aside.

"I am called—"

A chime sounded—the half-*kwatrane* warning to translation end. Cantra moved a hand.

"Quickly, your name. I must to the tower in a heartbeat."

One wild brow lifted, imperious.

"I am Sartony Tokai of House Tan Jevonese," the woman said. "I am valuable. Return me and be rewarded beyond your dreams of wealth."

Author Commentary

I LOVE THIS SPLINTER: "Strings, strands, and vines in motion"!

Why, you ask?

Omighod, where to start?

OK—first, it has Cantra; who is one of my favorite characters to write.

Second—it has Cantra's brother, Pleny, he who, in *Crystal Soldier*, struck a teacher and thereby caused 'way more trouble than he could ever have been expecting.

Third—it has that spaceport! That world! The smartstrands!

Fourth—it has wine! and the mother of the vine!

Fifth—oh, no, that's enough. Let's just say that I love this splinter, and I'm really glad I found it when I was cleaning out all those blessed typescripts.

I hope you enjoy reading this one as much as I did. If you did, please consider donating—to Cantra, to the site, or to the author who has just filled up six big black trash bags with old typescripts.

Sharon Lee

January 6, 2003

First Pass: Scout's Progress

Aelliana Caylon laughed out loud as her craft hit the shuttle webbing. Dead-center: a Master Pilot could have done no better, truth spoken. *Ge'shada, Junior Pilot,* she congratulated herself heartily. *Perhaps you should study for that First Class, after all.*

She laughed again, fingers busy at the straps. Her mother would be mortified, of course. Mizel was a clan of scholars:theorists, not experimentalists. Her position in the Mathematics Department of the University of Liad barely atoned for her Second Class Pilot's license. Nothing she had yet achieved in her area of specialty balanced the fact that she preferred to pilot herself and did so at every opportunity.

Chuckling from sheer good spirits, she rolled out of the tiny craft and dropped lightly to the ground. She glanced at the fence separating the sheds from the shuttlepads involuntarily, expecting to be disappointed—and nearly laughed again. She was able to avoid *that* impropriety, though the grin that split her face would have called a rebuke from her delm.

"There you are!" she cried, nearly skipping to the fence and the slim figure perched atop it.

"Why," he said, looking down at his leathered self in surprise, "so I am. My thanks to you, Lady. I had been in a fair way to believing myself misplaced."

She did laugh then, but quickly sobered. "And who has said to you that I am called 'Lady'?"

"It is true,is it not? Lady Aelliana Caylon. Of Clan Mizel."

"But this is monstrous! I don't know *your* name, after all."

"It was a well-executed landing,just now," he said, ignoring this rather blatant hint. "I'm pleased that I was able to witness it. Have you considered training for the next class? You'd do well, I think."

"Do you?" She was pleased, more so since their previous discussions had shown her that he was himself no poor pilot. "It is good to hear you say so. And good to see you again. You were gone such a time, I was certain you'd found better wages at another port."

The leathers and the gloves he always wore marked a person who worked in the shuttlesheds a mechanic, most likely; and pilot-to-hire.

"Ah, well," he said, moving his shoulders. "My skills were in demand at another location for a time and I could not come away." He smiled. "That I was missed—Lady, you give me hope. Perhaps we might dine?"

"Yes, certainly! When I know neither your name nor clan, while you know all of me!"

"Surely not *all*?"He tipped his head. "It might be arranged."

She sighed, tempted; bowed denial. "I think it unlikely,smile-friend. I am sorry." This was walking rather too close to the line between propriety and scandal. Her mother would have blushed for her, had she been present.

"Are you? Then I am *certain* it might be done. Trust me."

Abruptly, he slid to the ground on the far side of the fence.

"Be well, Lady. Until our next meeting."

"Until our next meeting," she echoed; then turned resolutely toward the lot and her groundcar.

HANLEN CAYLON, DELM Mizel, sat at her desk, eyes on the contract she had long since read and re-read. Korval was mad, of course—they'd been so from the beginning. However, the gentleman who had so recently quitted her office was not mad; nor did one refuse such an offer from the most powerful of all Liad's clans. At least, she amended to herself, not without substantive reason.

Aelliana had done her duty once, providing Mizel with a child of her body, as required by both law and tradition. She would do her duty again. Indeed, it was this business of providing one's clan with an heir that brought Korval to Mizel at all.

A light step outside the door proceeded a shadow across her light. She looked up, frowning at the leather jacket and helter-skelter hair. Really, the child could take a *semblance* of care...

"You wished to see me, Mother?"

Hanlon Caylon brought her attention firmly to the present.

"Yes, Aelliana. Sit, if you please."

She did so and folded her hands quietly. Delm Mizel's frown deepened as she let her eyes rove over the merely brown hair, the thin face with its straight brows and greenish eyes. Her fingers moved on the vellum beneath them. The contract specified *Aelliana, second child of Line Caylon, Philosopher of Mathematics and Pilot, Second Class.*

Hanlen sighed, tapped her finger against the sheaf and cleared her throat.

"Mizel has been approached by Clan Korval," she said flatly, "in the matter of contract-marriage."

Aelliana's face showed polite interest, and perhaps a bit of puzzlement. She waited, as was proper.

"Mizel feels," the delm continued, "that it is in the best interest of the clan to pursue such a liaison with Korval at this time (*or at any other*, she added to herself)." She looked at her daughter sharply."The contract *will be* signed."

Still Aelliana waited, hands quiescent in her lap.

Hanlen sighed, and tapped the vellum again."It is Delm Korval himself who seeks to give his clan an heir. The one of Mizel he honors by his attention is Aelliana Caylon."

There were many things she could have done: she might have cried out that she knew the man and despised him. Or she might have preened herself on her unlooked-for good fortune. She might have inclined her head dutifully and awaited further instruction from her mother and her delm.

She should not have laughed.

"Have taken leave of your senses?" demanded Mizel, awfully.

Aelliana fought for control; won a brief respite.

"It is—Mother, don't you see?They must have mistaken the name. Of course it must be *Elian*, and not Aelliana at all!"

Well, Mizel acknowledged, and so she too had thought, at first. Who better to give Korval his heir than the elder daughter: beautiful, well mannered, polished? She looked at her youngest with something close to approval.

"Korval's man of business brought this to me himself, and we sat and discussed the matter in all of its ramifications. The name is correct." She swallowed and forbore to glare at the leather jacket. "He asked that the matter be presented to you when you returned from the port."

Aelliana stared. "*Presented* to me?"

Hanlen recalled that she had not yet uncovered the whole. "Delm Korval would be pleased to be introduced to you *before* signatures are set to swear-lines. It was thought he might attend Prime meal with us tomorrow evening."

"I see." The greenish eyes were a little vague, thought Hanlen, though the child answered reasonably enough.

"I would be pleased to meet with Delm Korval before the contract is signed. If it is convenient for him to attend Prime tomorrow, then, of course, I shall be present."

It was a dutiful, and irreproachably proper answer.

Hanlen Caylon regarded her daughter warily.

"You will of course allow yourself to be guided by your mother and your sister in the matters of dress and mode."

"Of course," Aelliana agreed, still with that unfocused look about her.

"Good," said the delm, with forced heartiness. "Then I will tell you that it would be useful for you to utilize the sleep-enchancement tapes this night. I shall myself program the proper sections of the Code into the unit."

No protest was forthcoming. Hanlen cleared her throat.

"Have you questions, child?"

"No, Mother."

"You may go, then. Please send your sister to me."

"Yes, Mother."

She was gone.

ANOTHER MARRIAGE, GODS?

Aelliana had been married once, as all must be; and had given the clan a fine son. She saw him now and again, when his nurse allowed. He did not seem to find her interesting or necessary to his comfort in any way. His father in him, no doubt.

His father had been an honorable man.Dull and worthy, he had joined with her family in deploring her ambition toward a pilot's license; had professed himself scandalized to learn that she had actually won *Moreta* in a game of dice. She had neglected to tell him from whom she had won the ship, though she had several times been tempted.

And now here was Korval—honorable, no doubt. Worthy, of course.Dull? But most people were dull, after all. Gods, why *her*? There was Elian, who would be knife-tongued in envy; who was more suited to stand wife to the most powerful man on the planet. . .

She would have to take leave from the University, of course; put aside half-formed, enticing plans for a vacation off-planet; place *Moreta* in storage...

Aelliana flumped into the dowdy, lumpy chair by the window in her room and glared out at the inner court waters.Not to mention the obligatory beddings and intercourse, which bored her.Another person's hands on putting you *here* and then *there*—Pah! She could make no sense of people who took pleasure-love after pleasure-love. A monumental waste of time, and love no pleasure, at all.

Still, she acknowledged some while later, duty counted and the clan had not been brutal in its use of her.It was generally acknowledged that she was the odd one and then the matter was usually let drop.If he were not too dull, this Delm Korval—but, of course, he would be.

Sighing, Aelliana got up to dress for Prime.

ONCE AGAIN, SHE STOOD in front of the mirror, manicured hands stroking the yellow silk of the new gown. It became her well—Elian's eye was unerring, even enlisted in a cause she declared hopeless. The several rings on her fingers were loaned from her mother, saving only the plain, intricately woven silver band she always wore on the second finger of her left hand. That one looked a little dowdy, in fact, against the gleaming splendor of her mother's gems, but she did not take it off. She had worn it so long it was like a part of her hand; she might as easily left off a thumb.

The clock on her dresser chimed, and she gave the dress one last stroke before going belowstairs to meet the guests.

THE ROOM SEEMED UNREASONABLY crowded. Aelliana hesitated on the threshold, sleep-lessons and commonsense deserting her, it seemed. How *did* one address a delm of another clan? A six-year-old might have told her—and Aelliana would have been glad of the answer.

Her mother was coming toward her, regal in dark red; a tall, slender young man on her arm. She was smiling and chatting determinedly. So much Aelliana saw before her attention was captured once more by her mother's escort.

Tall, yes, and slender, moving with a smooth elegance that cried *pilot*, and the silence that whispered *scout*. Dark hair, dark eyes, high cheeks and generous mouth...

"Delm Korval, this is Lady Aelliana Caylon, Clan Mizel," her mother was saying formally while Aelliana stared into the man's face.

He bowed—the bow between equals, Aelliana saw, through thawing shock.

"Lady Aelliana, I am happy to meet you."

"Aelliana," her mother's voice carried an undercurrent of sternness. "This is Daav yos'Phelium, Delm Korval."

"Delm Korval," she murmured, returning the bow exactly, "I am happy to see you."

Her mission accomplished. Delm Mizel withdrew. Daav yos'Phelium grinned down at her, the exact and, let her say it, beloved grin of her friend of the airfield.

"Now," he said, "did I not *say* that it might be arranged?"

Author Commentary

ONE OF THE THINGS THAT an author must learn early, and practice often, is: Always Trust the Back-Brain.

Not too far, naturally, or too literally, but Just Enough. Because the Back-Brain is right far, far more often than it is wrong.

A case in point is presented in the. . .let's call it *the outline* for the novel that became *Scout's Progress*. I often outline by writing snippets of what's going to happen in a particular novel. As the years have gone by, I've actually developed the ability to write the snippets in more-or-less the order that they'll appear in the novel—which is endlessly helpful, and saves having to push all the furniture in the living room to the walls, so I can kneel down with the printed-out snippets and deal them across the rug, until the correct order has been established.

The. . .outline for *Scout's Progress*, though. . .that came 'way out of order.

We think.

Let me briefly outline the situation.

We've been writing a long, long time. *Agent of Change* and the first draft of *Conflict of Honors* were written on a typewriter, starting back in, oh, 1984. *Carpe Diem* was the first book we wrote completely on a computer—a Kaypro so-called "portable" computer, running the ancient and revered operating system known as CP/M. I think we got the Kaypro in 1986, when the on-acceptance check for *Agent* cleared the bank. At the same time, we bought a nine-pin printer.

Now, during the time we were writing *Agent of Change, Conflict of Honors* and *Carpe Diem*, we were also thinking about Where The Story Was Going. And I—it was almost always me, since Steve's back-brain is organized differently, plus? He has a really good memory.—I would be struck by An Idea, A Scene, A Character—and I would rush to write it down.

In those days, we saved things on 5.25 inch floppies, but nobody really trusted them. We—I, anyhow—still printed things out, as a back-up, because who knew what the new-fangled tech would do, this time tomorrow, while a file drawer? Was *forever*.

Well. . .not exactly forever. Because. . .printouts made on 9-pin dot matrix printers to 18-lb burst computer paper? Fade. Not, I'll grant, as *quickly* as printouts made onto thermal paper, but fade they do.

I found this out yesterday, when, as fate would have it, I unearthed an old free-standing file holder full of old files, which I intended to throw out, so that the holder could be re-purposed to hold the files of the new projects we're working on.

Except that, when I opened the files, I found—scene after scene after scene, printed faithfully out on that poor old 9-pin printer, which must have ascended directly to heaven when its time came, given the hell the two of us put it through.

To the best of my knowledge, given the printer, the rediscovered scenes were written in 1986/1987—before, in fact, Steve and I moved to Maine, because we didn't bring the printer with us to Maine—we sold it, along with my blue Depression glass, for gas money.

So it looks like, in 1986/87? My brain was *on fire*. I have here a scene where Pat Rin has found the *Passage* after having been offered the Ring by a stranger. I have another scene with Val Con and Miri, after he was re-taken by the DOI. Another—a short conversation between Daav and Val Con regarding Val Con's probable chance of survival, should Miri die. Ideas for stories that became novels, lists of words, character descriptions. . .

. . .and this snippet—the first outline for *Scout's Progress*.

Now, I happen to love this outline. I love that—though it gets *so many* things wrong—it gets the important stuff right.

Aelliana is the odd child in her clan—check.

She doesn't know who her new friend is—check.

She doesn't want to be married again—check.

I love, love, love that she *already* has her grandmother's puzzle ring.

And that she's teaching mathematics at the university.

And that she had *always* won her ship in a game of chance, and from a person so unsavory, she hesitates to say his name.

Daav is hanging out for a wife—check.

He's sneaky from the get-go—the *very first time* I wrote Daav yos'Phelium and the back-brain gets him *exactly right*! Go, back-brain!

. . .of course, there are all those things that the back-brain got wrong. Had I written out from what's there, taking *all of it* literally, it would have...well. A very different book.

I'm happy with the book we did eventually write, and I'm thrilled to have found this intact first attempt at an outline.

I hope you'll enjoy it.

Sharon Lee
October 12, 2011

Four Tries for an Yxtrang

One

It was twilight when the big man finally gave over and began to shut the equipment down for the night.

A somewhat smaller man, snugged down among the ferns under the shadowy embrace of the trees, grinned carefully, keeping his head well down. He had recently fought a similar battle with his own instruments, squandering a whole day in an agony of patience, re-calibrating, fine-tuning and cleaning—only to net another gaggle of absurd readings.

The second day he had yielded to his own impetuous nature, damned the instruments and the handbook in blunt Terran and stalked off to do a manual survey and soil sample, after which the instruments performed just as they ought.

The big man really should take a soil sample.

He showed no disposition to do so, however; merely going about the business of getting his instruments properly stowed, his artistically scarred face showing nothing in the lemony after-light but a certain stoic intelligence.

The small watcher nestled his chin on a leather-clad forearm, green eyes watching the scene in the clearing with a sort of drowsy intensity.

The big man's stoicism was not surprising. Neither, though it ran contrary to beliefs dear to the collective heart of the watcher's home culture, was the obvious intelligence with which he went about his duties.

What did surprise were the duties he so diligently pursued, mirroring as they did duties the watcher himself was charged to perform.

The Liaden Scouts, an organization in which the watcher held the rank of Captain, First In, owned what was perhaps the most comprehensive library of Yxtrang lore in the galaxy. It was fitting, after all, that so ancient and terrible an enemy be studied with the respect centuries of predation must engender. It to be deplored that such determined study had yet to yield the final secret of Yxtrang vulnerability, but this had little bearing on the difficulty now facing the Scout Captain.

For all he had learned regarding the Yxtrang showed them to be a race of soldiers, pirates prone to coming locust-like to planets already settled and proven, driving out or killing the settlers or native population and claiming the world for their Never, in all the years Yxtrang and Liadens had chased each other among the stars, had there been any hint that Yxtrang had scouts. Yet here was one, performing recognizably scout-like duties with a mien and forebearance expectable from all but the most ill-disciplined of young captains—alone, unwarlike ...accessible.

The young captain experienced a thrill, quickly damped. If Yxtrang had scouts...

The big man had finished stowing his equipment. He bent and picked up his pack, slipping the straps over arms the size of the smaller man's thighs. He settled the load, turned toward the clearing's opposite side—and paused, head cocked as if he had heard, below the racket of bird calls and tree-groan, the natter of the watching scout's thought.

The young captain froze, breath trapped deep in his chest,eyes drawn irresistibly to the Yxtrang's utility belt and the wicked curve of the grace-blade hanging there. In the deep forest behind him, the first lizard of the evening coughed and gave tongue.

The Yxtrang shrugged his wide shoulders and turned away.

The scout gulped breath, waited for the count of two hundred, then flitted silently across the clearing and into the wood opposite, trailing his enemy back to camp.

DAWN FOUND HIM AT ANOTHER certain place, crouching in the lee of a black-and-purple shrub, the end of a rope tied to the roots at his feet. The rest of the tight-stretched length angled sharply upward, vanishing into the dense vegetation over his head.

His arrangements had long since been made, and he only awaited the advent of the Yxtrang—of the *Yxtrang scout*. Yes.

Well, and it remained to be seen what a Liaden scout might accomplish against the ancient racial enemy.

Observation over three days had shown that the Yxtrang came to this place every morning at dawn to check his traps and harvest his breakfast, Yxtranq regulations apparently not being as stringent as Liaden regarding the ingestion of alien foodstuffs. The Yxtrang would soon learn the danger of keeping too particular a schedule on an unknown world, where an unsuspected sentience might well be spying upon one and all one's affairs.

The scout captain checked his own utility belt, fingers straying from pellet gun to the woodclad stick-knife. He slid the knife free and flicked it open and shut so quickly the blade blurred in a snag of silver, and smiled. It was not so grand a weapon as the Yxtrang's grace-blade, but it would serve. It would serve.

A rustle not of the wind's making warned him and he ducked close to his bush as the Yxtrang came along the path with a grace astonishing in so large a creature. He paused at the first of his traps and grunted in satisfaction at the still-wriggling small-life caught there. He wrung its neck with calm efficiency and hung the carcass from a hook in his belt before bending and resetting the lure.

Trap rigged for dinner, he continued down the path, passing close enough for the scout to smell the odor of gun oil and soap, and was gone, four steps, six steps, seven ...eight ...

"Hai!"

The tree snapped skyward, dragging the Yxtrang, feet first and swearing, toward the murky clouds.

"Hai!" the scout cried, echoing the other's cry as the sticknife gleamed downward, parting the rope in one clean stroke.

The second and third trees whipped high, launching net and binding strings as the scout came half-erect by his bush, grinning like the boy he was; in fact, nearly laughing. Except it was no laughing matter, the quickness with which the Yxtrang understood his situation. One try he made for grace-blade and belt through the tangle of the vine-woven net; one attempt to gain control of the rope's swing; then he was still, patient as a rock.

But not quite rocklike. As the scout watched, the huge muscles in the Yxtrang's shoulders tightened, testing the coils pinning his arms to his chest, concentration and feral intelligence showing in the tatooed face.

The scout gulped against a sudden sweep of lightheaded nausea and touched, as if for assurance, not only the skinny stickknife, but the other blades, as well. He was right, he assured himself firmly and came to his full, meagre heiqht there by the bush.

He was right. The enemy of his people hung a dozen steps away, powerless, awaiting his will.

He *was* right.

Firmly, he stepped out into the path and walked out to work his will.

Two

EGRETH BATTALION STORMENG Company Ilpraz Unit Fourth Soldier Detached, Nelirikk proceeded cautiously through the tall trees, skirting clammy hanging vines and upthrust roots. This was an ancient place, peopled it seemed by mere animals, rather than animals with weapons. Thus far, then, it was well.

Underbrush now, and a slight thinning of trunk and vine. Nelirikk paused at the edge of the clearing, cautious in spite of the lack of man-spoor.

Grid by grid, he studied the place, noting that the pinkish grass stood unmarred. Nothing had passed this way for quite some time. Excellent. He would rest here, eat, consider where next to travel on this world he meant to claim for Yxtrang.

Satisfied, he straightened and strode across the grass. It hissed past his ears and pinned his arms to his sides before he had a chance to react. Startled, he jerked his arms outward, meaning to snap the puny thing, only to find it tightening, lifting.

He roared and fought, legs churning fruitlessly as the thing had its way with him and he was suspended nearly a foot above the crushed and broken lawn.

Dangling, he looked about him. The clearing was empty. A glance downward showed the thing that held him captive: a supple, wire-thin rope. His guns hung on his belt, and his grace blade. But he could not reach them.

Captive! There was only one creature so lost to honor that it imprisoned its enemy, rather than offering clean death.

"Terran!" Nelirikk roared, swinging gently to and fro at the end of his rope. "Come out, thing, and let a warrior see a coward!"

Silence in the glade. Nelirikk struggled to reach his blade and began to describe a ragged arc.

"Terran!"

"No Terrans here, *Chrackek* Yxtrang."

Nelirikk searched the clearing for the owner of that soft voice; turned his head too sharply to see behind and added a twirl to the arc.

"It might go better," commented the voice gently, "if you were to hang loosely and allow the motion to still. A suggestion only, you understand. Far from me is the ordering of so mighty a warrior as yourself."

"Stand out, animal!"

"As you will."

No leaf moved. No branch rustled. Across the clearing a small man, spaceleathered and toolbelted, simply *was*.

"Liaden!" Nelirikk spat and the rope shivered.

The little man bowed. "*Chrachek* Yxtrang."

"Why do you hesitate, Liaden? Slay me."

"Ah," murmured the little man, coming silently across the grass. "I thought perhaps we might speak."

"Speak? I am an honorable man. What should I say to an animal?"

"You seem to have said several things already," his captor pointed out. "It is possible you might find something else, given a few moments to consider and form your thoughts. Or, I might ask you a question or two and you might answer. This process is called 'conversation.'"

"Conversation," sneered Nelirikk, giving no sign of the concern that began to shape in him. Obviously, this Liaden was rabid. It had always been the case between Yxtrang and Liaden that one slew the other. No other way was possible. Terrans. . .Terrans took prisoners among the Yxtrang. Terrans—especially those called 'Aus'—questioned under duress. It was told that Liadens and Terrans cross-bred now and again. Perhaps this one had Terran blood in it, and thus was mad.

"Conversation," agreed the little man, seating himself on the grass a few feet from where Nelirikk hung, impotent.

"An exchange of ideas—perhaps even an exchange of information. For an instance, my name is Val Con yos'Phelium, Scout Captain." He paused, then prompted softly. "Now, you might tell me your name,

Three

STAREG BATTALION GRED Company Exbolg Unit Detached Soldier Exploratory Nelirikk walked carefully beneath the trees. They were old trees, sky-high; looped with ropy brown vines along the lowest branches.

Nelirikk bent low, careful of the vines in spite of the throat guard he wore. They seemed harmless—like the trees—but one never knew.

A clearing presented itself. Nelirikk crouched, taking advantage of the scant brush; quartered the area in his mind's eye and examined each quarter before again carefully considering the whole.

No signs of habitation. No signs of laid traps. No sign of danger—manmade or natural. Apparently, it was safe to continue.

Nelirikk remained in position, eyes slitted, nostrils distended as he tasted the essence of the clearing. This was not a technique his superiors had instructed him in. Rather, it was something he had heard in a story, about the fires when he was made part of the Boy's Troop. The tale was of the Smallest Soldier and how he had kept his life and the lives of all his Troop by taking but a moment longer to "test the air' and listen to nothing in particular.

Four

EGRETH BATTALION STORMENG Company Ilpraz Unit Fourth Soldier Detached, Nelirikk proceeded cautiously through the tall trees, skirting clammy hanging vines and upthrust roots. This was an ancient place, peopled it seemed by mere animals, rather than animals with weapons. Thus far, then, it was well.

Underbrush now, and a slight thinning of trunk and vine. Nelirikk paused at the edge of the clearing, cautious in spite of the lack of man-spoor.

Grid by grid, he studied the place, noting that the pinkish grass stood unmarred. Nothing had passed this way for quite some time. Excellent. He would rest here, eat, consider where next to travel on this world he meant to claim for Yxtrang.

Satisfied, he straightened and strode across the grass.

It hissed past his ears and pinned his arms to his sides before he had a chance to react. Startled, he jerked his arms outward, meaning to snap the puny thing, only to find it tightening, lifting.

He roared and fought, legs churning fruitlessly as the thing had its way with him and he was suspended nearly a foot above the crushed and broken lawn.

Dangling, he looked about him. The clearing was empty. A glance downward showed the thing that held him captive: a supple, wire-thin rope. His guns hung on his belt, and his grace blade. But he could not reach them.

Captive! There was only one creature so lost to honor that it imprisoned its enemy, rather than offering clean death.

"Terran!" Nelirikk roared, swinging gently to and fro at the end of his rope. "Come out, thing, and let a warrior see a coward!"

Silence in the glade. Nelirikk struggled to reach his blade and began to describe a ragged arc.

"Terran!"

"No Terrans here, *Chrackek* Yxtrang."

Nelirikk searched the clearing for the owner of that soft voice; turned his head too sharply to see behind and added a twirl to the arc.

"It. might go better," commented the voice gently, "if you were to hang loosely and allow the motion to still. A suggestion only, you understand. Far from me is the ordering of so mighty a warrior as yourself."

"Stand out, animal!"

"As you will."

No leaf moved. No branch rustled. Across the clearing a small man, spaceleathered and toolbelted, simply *was*.

"Liaden!" Nelirikk spat and the rope shivered.

The little man bowed . "Chrackek Yxtrang."

Author Commentary

THE ABOVE IS A RARE look at process, which was found in the recent Scouring of the Files referenced earlier.

I presented the snippets above in the order in which they were found in the file folder. No, I don't know if the segment on the top was written last, first, or simultaneous with the others, which were clipped together in the order presented.

Steve suggests that he is responsible for the segments told from Nelirikk's POV, while I am to be blamed for Val Con. Which hardly seems fair, and in any case is another argument altogether.

One note—The text below is reproduced exactly as it appears on the page (with the exception of various stains, which might be coffee, or cocoa, or Something More Sinister). This means, yes—typos, spelling mistakes, and at least one section that stops in the middle of a sentence, directly after a ",".

We found these bits of flotsam from the past Rather Amusing, and hope you will, too.

Sharon Lee

When Val Con was re-attached to the DOI

N*ear end of the third? book...p. 1*
After that first quick glance at the gun, Miri never looked away from his face.

"Will you kill me now, Val Con?" she asked him softly, in Low Liaden.

She did not believe it. She had, he reflected, never believed it.

"That is the assignment," he said, in his clear, accentless Terran. "Will you fight me?"

"Fight you, *cha'trez*? I could never lay a hand on you, unless you let me. Kill me, if you must..." She tipped her head. "I would ask a boon, however."

"Ask," he said, never moving the gun.

"Do you still have your clan blade, *cha'trez*?"

Straight brows twitched together in a frown. "Of course."

"Of course," she echoed the Terran words, then returned to Low Liaden. "Then I ask you to kill me with it." She took a deep breath and squared her shoulders. "It is my right as a clan member to die by the blade of a kinsman."

He looked at her. Valiant Miri. Then he shook his head, minding the tick of the inner clock. It grew late.

"Come close, then," he told her.

She covered the distance between them in six firm strides and stood looking up; her throat a sweet, unprotected curve. He moved his eyes to her face. She met his gaze squarely and he saw that she was crying.

"Why do you weep" he asked her, returning the gun to its holster. "Are you afraid?"

"I love you, Val Con," she said, singing the Low Liaden words. And then in Terran. "I love you. Now do what you will."

Edger's knife was in his hand, she saw the flash of it. She forced herself to look only into his eyes, clear and green and utterly without expression.

Quickly, she thought, feeling her courage begin to fail. Lest he see, she closed her eyes—

And was hit by a force that sent her spinning across the room, pinned to the floor by the body atop her. There was warm breath in her ear.

The noise of the explosion sent her to the threshold of unconsciousness; the wild twisting of the floor brought her back.

When all was quiet, she lay still beneath the man who held her, waiting for the cold bite of crystal.

"I love you, Miri," came the Low Liaden words in her ear. "Valiant, courageous and strong. *Cha'trez*; beloved lifemate..."

She took a breath, daring to shift, just a little.

"Val Con?" disbelieving.

"Yes." He moved, rolling clear of her and coming to his knees, gun in hand. Pointed out, covering the wrecked room.

Twisting, she sat on the ruined floor, watching the side of his face. "What did they do to you?"

He turned his head to smile at her. "I don't know," he said, "I didn't listen..."

She waved her hand in a large gesture. "All that was an act?"

"Forgive me," he murmured, watching her face, "It did seem best."

She sighed, rolling to her feet. "Remind me to break your jaw."

Author Commentary

THE ABOVE SPLINTER comes from the "Pieces" file that gave us the first draft of *Scout's Progress*.

It's not dated, but I'm calling 1984, for two reasons: (1) the scene was *typed* and (2) the notation at the top of the page reads: *near end of the third? book...p.1* Which says to me that it was written either during or directly after we finished writing *Agent of Change*.

The writing's a little cheesy, though the punch line is pure Miri. Still, not too bad for baby writers who were trying to feel out a potential confrontation, and trying to see what hooks they might have to plant.

What interests me most as one of the author/creators is recalling that Steve and I had known going in that, at some point in the story arc, the Department of the Interior would reacquire Val Con and point him at Korval. That was a given.

Later, we considered that perhaps Miri might be acquired, as a hostage, but role-playing proved to us that this strategy would leave the DOI with a dead hostage and Val Con free, in command of Korval's considerable resources, and bent on Balance.

That scenario would have been *interesting*, given that Miri is the keeper of Val Con's soul, and without her he's no better than he was, but, ultimately, we're not the kind of writer who enjoys working in a pitch-black tunnel, without even the light of an onrushing locomotive to hearten us.

Also, things—history, geography, relationships, the universe—changed around and under us as we went forward with the story. Val Con and Miri revealed themselves to be lifemates in the old sense of a Wizard's Match; that meant they both suddenly had available to them resources that we hadn't, err, *known about*, going in.

Still, the *DOI* didn't know about the lifemate bond, and recapturing Val Con would greatly increase their chances of success in the Big Game of Galactic Domination—they were bound to try it.

So, we worked on, bearing this important, and inevitable plot point in mind; and it was determined, in the way that writers determine things, that the DOI would make its move in *Plan B*.

. . .and that's where the book stalled. I was lead writer on *Plan B*, and I must've written 50,000 words of scenes setting up Val Con recapture—none of which worked. I spent some time under the desk—this is true; I sometimes will sit under my desk if a story has stalled, to get a Different Perspective—I took long walks; Steve and I role-played. . .

Nothing worked.

Nothing worked.

As Shan mentions in his comments to Nova, Val Con and Miri are by the time Plan B rolls out, extremely dangerous people. Also? Val Con made it quite plain that he would far rather die than return to the care of the DOI. . .

. . .and Miri was on-board with that plan.

In the end, we did find a way for Val Con to be retaken by the DOI that was believable and in keeping with who he and Miri had become together—and even incorporated that business about "wanting, rather, to die..."

. . .but it wasn't what we had envisioned—*what we knew had to happen from day one* —and it was mostly to salve our auctorial pride.

Now, you may, with some justice, be asking yourselves, *Why is she telling us this?*

The reason is to remind us—*all of us*—that stories that are true, are also fluid; nothing is certain; everything is on the table; anything is possible.

I know that some people don't feel comfortable just "writing out of their heads"; they want to know what happens before they Get There, so they don't get lost, or wander too far astray of the story. Given the number of times we've gotten to a Certain Place in a novel and the author-days we then spent beating our heads against What Happens Next?, I can't really advise anyone *not* to plot.

But I can say. . .be flexible, be aware that, as the characters move across the story-space, they change—themselves, the plot, and sometimes even the thrust of the story. Certainly, they change their authors.

Daav's Up Early

Jelaza Kazone
Surebleak

He woke before the birds, head buzzing with a scheme for sponsoring a junior course.

The number of secondary school scholars seeking to audit such subjects as traveler's etiquette, language diversity, and other hands-on tertiary courses had grown significantly since he had first taken the Gallowglass Chair. He had been thinking for some time that there was not only room, but demand, for a team-level course in kinesics. Of course, Admin would never allow *him* to teach it, deeming it beneath the dignity of a Scholar Expert to instruct children. However, there was to hand Donet, one of his advanced students. He was concerned of Donet, who had the material more thoroughly than any other of his advisees, yet who continued to mistrust his instincts at every turn. Teaching those who were truly ignorant would cement his knowledge, and the gain in confidence—

Yes, he thought; it would do. He would bring it to the Registrar this very morning, and present the thing to Donet as an accomplished fact.

He was thoroughly awake now; energized, and not likely to go back to sleep. Best to rise, then, gently, so as not to rouse Kamele...

Daav yos'Phelium Clan Korval opened his eyes.

He was alone in the wide bed. The carved chest against the wall just there would have fit into the shared bedroom at Number Twelve Leafydale Place only with the sacrifice of the bed. Nor had Jen Sar Kiladi possessed a jewel-box, much less one as handsome as that sitting atop the chest.

The testimony of the furniture placed him at Jelaza Kazone. He glanced up to the skylight, wondering at the dullness of the light. Was it so early, then?

But no. The skylight framed a cloudscape in sullen grey, occasionally enlivened by a spiteful spit of snow.

Memory finally came fully functional.

Jelaza Kazone had been relocated to Surebleak, and he had been returned to his clan.

Daav closed his eyes, abruptly without any necessity to rise. There was no Registrar with whom to do battle; no brilliant uncertain student to nurture. . .

No long-time, well-loved companion asleep next to him, half-curled on her side, pale hair as fine as feathers framing a long, intelligent face.

I miss her, too, Aelliana said, her voice seeming the veriest whisper in his ear.

"And soon we will miss Theo, as well," he said, grimly.

Theo will forgive us. His lifemate's voice was firm.

"Ah. As Val Con has forgiven us? Or Er Thom. Did he forgive us, Aelliana, when his lady was killed, his heart shattered, and his brother, who might have held him to life, was absent and uncaring?"

His answer was a profound silence, as weighty as it was brief.

I want to go for a walk.

He opened his eyes, so that she might observe the frowning sky.

"In that?"

Surely, we have walked in snow before. I wish to see the grounds, and what sort of country we have landed in.

There was, he admitted, something in what she said. One ought to know one's lands, after all, and such roads and trails and hidey-holes as might be available, at need.

And a walk would do them both good.

He threw back the blankets, came to his feet, and crossed the room to the closet.

THE FORMAL GARDENS at the front of the house had survived the journey, though it remained to be seen if they would survive Surebleak.

It was chill enough that Daav turned up the collar of his jacket as he paused on the path to take his bearings.

In. . .other days, he would have walked to the right of the house, to the place where the formal gardens gave way to the working land. At that point, he would have turned to follow long rows of vegetables, soil monitors twinkling among the leaves like stars. Eventually, he would have entered a slender belt of trees and found a path tending uphill, which he would follow until the trees thinned and he stepped out onto Trealla Fantrol's spacious lawns.

This morning, he turned to the left, and strode out briskly, hands tucked into his pockets, the sense of Aelliana's presence so strong that it seemed he must certainly see her gamely keeping pace beside him, if he but turned his head a fraction.

He had long ago learnt that bitter lesson; and kept his eyes straight ahead.

"Aelliana," he said, his breath frosting the chill air.

Van'chela?

"I wonder if I might now prevail upon you to tell me why you felt it. . .necessary that we form an alliance with Kamele Waitley?"

It was an old question; and though he could—and had—guessed at her reasons, she had steadfastly refused to state them. He expected another refusal this morning; indeed, what matter did it make, now?

There was a long pause as he walked on, occasionally assaulted by a snowflake, before Aelliana spoke, surprisingly, and perhaps not quite as firmly as she might have wished.

Necessity.

Well, but that was only what any well-brought-up Liaden might say when confronted with a demand for an explanation she did not wish to give. He had his refusal, after all.

But—no. It seemed that, this morning, Aelliana had something more to say on his topic.

You will. . . perhaps think me deficient in the order of my duty, she continued, slowly. After all, the ship is the care of the pilot and the co-pilot's care is the pilot. However, our order became reversed when we came into our present arrangement. Surely, you are the pilot of your own body, and the course lain in for Balance arose from your genuis.

That being so, I took up my care, and it came to my attention that my pilot. . .required. . .more stimulus than he was likely to gain in solitude, even a solitude leavened by students, and cats, and a voice only he could hear.

I therefore set out to provide my pilot with human contact. You may ask 'why Kamele?'—but that you may answer for yourself, van'chela. I saw that she interested you; that she was a scholar, and out of the common way. She had a strong, trained mind and a resolute spirit—both attributes required in a long-term companion. For it would not have done, you know, Daav, to have taken up with someone you could bully.

That surprised a laugh out of him, even as his eye snagged on an...irregularity in the land ahead.

Cautiously, he approached the ragged edge where the formal garden formed a uneasy border with what seemed to be a crack in the land.

The edge of the old mine pit? Aelliana wondered.

"So it would seem. We have not been an exact match, which should surprise no one."

He felt the ripple of her laughter as he approached the irregularity, wary of sinkholes and disturbed rocks.

The space that separated the land that had accompanied Jelaza Kazone and native Surebleak dirt was not wide—even an elderly, desk-bound scholar might easily make the leap—nor was it particularly deep, perhaps extending to a depth matching Daav's height. It had been Edger's avowed intent to plant house and tree firmly, whereupon the Tree, so it had said, would see to the rooting of things.

In time, the gully between the worlds would fill, Daav thought, nor was the pit into which they had been settled a wound of Korval's making. Still, it might be best to begin their tenure here with healing. And one would not like to think of a child, or an unwary adult, or a rabbit, tumbling into the crack and taking harm.

Daav raised his head.

The land across the divide had the look of being tended and worked, for all its lack of crisp lines and the busy flashings of monitors. His eye marked out rows, newly raked, and there, leaning against a wizened tree bearing some small, pink fruits along its twisted branches, the rake itself.

. . .beyond the rake, tucked not-quite-behind the trunk, obscured by the branches, was a man. A long, thin man, with a cap pulled low over a brown face. Dark blonde hair stuck out around the cap, like straw out of a hay-rick. An eye gleamed in the shadows; blinked.

Daav settled on his heels, bringing his attention—and Aelliana's—once more to the study of the crack.

"The question is," he said, conversationally, "what to fill it with. Gravel? 'crete? Stumps?"

"Dirt," a rough voice said from nearer than he would have thought likely. Their new neighbor moved on his own land like a scout. Daav hadn't heard the disturbance of so much as a blade of grass.

Once again, he raised his head.

Across the gully, and somewhat further removed from it than Daav was on his side, a man squatted on his heels. His clothes were rough, but well-mended and clean. The brown eyes that watched him out of the shadow made by the cap's peak were wary to the point of being feral.

"Good morning," Daav said, pleasantly, but without any needless emphasis.

The man nodded, jerkily, bony fingers gripping his own ankles. "Morning. Name's Shaper—Yulian—Yulie Shaper. I hold the land here." He looked down, as if to emphasize which land, exactly, he meant.

"I am glad to meet you, Yulie Shaper," Daav said. "My name is Daav yos'Phelium."

The man gave another one of his jerky nods. "You're Boss Conrad's Da."

"I am Boss Conrad's uncle," Daav corrected, gently. He glanced to the gully. "So you think dirt alone will seal this?"

"Could put riprap—that's your gravel. Take a might of it, though, and the likeliest gravel pit in these parts is underneath where you're setting."

"Ah. I see that we may have been hasty."

Yulie Shaper frowned slightly and shook his head, as if levity were a pesky insect worrying at his ears.

"Problem with stumps is they rot and crumble up, so's you gotta keep hauling in more. 'crete. . .that might work, same as riprap—but, see, nothing grows in rock. You wanna match up the edges, fill with dirt, then the grass'll grow the same on both sides. Hold it all together."

That, Daav suspected, was something of a burst of eloquence for Yulie Shaper. And a non-trivial effort it was; the man was breathing hard, as if he'd run a good, long distance.

"I think your advice is sound," he said, soothingly. "I wonder, though, how we would arrive at a quantity of dirt sufficient to the task. Have you any that you might wish to sell—or barter?"

Yulie Shaper frowned down at his land, brow furrowed. Daav waited, arms crossed on his knees.

"Melina," the man said abruptly.

He looked up at Daav and nodded once, decisively. "You want Melina Sherton. She's been moving a lot of dirt lately, on account of the new road." Another nod. "I got to go down her turf next day, two-day, for market. I could maybe let her know there's an interest."

"That would be. . .neighborly of you. I cannot commit Boss Korval, of course, but I will ask after intentions. When I have an answer, may I bring it to you—here? Or is there a place I might leave a note?"

"Gotta get the nod from the Boss, sure," Yulie Shaper said, coming to his feet in a lurch. "If I ain't obvious when you come 'cross here, leave a note up the house, on the door. I'll find it." He took a hard breath, seeming about to say something more. Daav kept to his crouch, looking toward, but not directly at, the other man's face.

"You don't hurt the cats," Yulie Shaper said finally.

"Indeed, no. I am very fond of cats; all of the family are."

It seemed that some of the tension left the man with that assurance, though by no means all of it. He nodded again—"That's good, then. Good cats, I got."—and without further ado, he spun on his heel and marched off, grabbing the rake from its lean against the tree as he went by.

Daav counted to thirty-six before rising, grimacing slightly at the complaint of stiff muscles.

"Well," he said lightly, to the grey sky, or to the spitting snow, or to his lifemate. "Perhaps we should go inside and find some tea."

Jelaza Kazone
Surebleak

IT WAS NOT, UPON INSPECTION, a very good road.

In point of fact, it was less a road and more a track the farther Yulie Shaper's land fell behind him. Daav walked along slowly, compiling mental notes in order that he might offer the fullest report possible to his delm. He also, so it seemed, walked alone; Aelliana had withdrawn from his awareness almost the instant he had stepped into the morning parlor in search of tea, to find his son and his son's lifemate at breakfast.

The children had been in spirits, and interested in news of their closest neighbor. Of the road a-building in Melina Sherton's territory, they were sanguine; it would appear that Boss Sherton had confided to Boss Conrad her vision of forging a route to the sea, which Daav thought, recalling his Surebleak geography, was an undertaking of no small ambition.

It pleased the delm to accept Yulie Shaper's neighborly offer to act as ambassador to Boss Sherton, and also to make Daav's return trip into double-duty. So after breakfast, saving a moment to write a note, should there be reason to have one, Daav had once again set off into the sullen day.

Yulie Shaper had not been "obvious" when he returned to their rendezvous point of the early morning. He paused a moment before making the minor leap over the gully, walking toward the gnarled tree with hands in plain view, and held slightly away from his body.

While not precisely a boulevard, the route "up" to the house made by the farmer in his rounds was obvious enough even to the eyes of an old scout. The weeds by the side of the path quivered from time to time, as if he were being paced, and he twice saw the gleam of cat-eyes among the straggling stems. No one approached him, though, either feline or human, and at last he came to the house, a tidy dwelling built of hardened wood.

Three steps rising to the door were rough-cut stone; the topmost adorned by a well-furred grey cat with upstanding ears, front legs tucked beneath white breast, eyes closed. Those strong ears twitched when Daav put his foot on the first step, and mint green eyes opened when he achieved the top. Apparently, he resembled neither dinner nor a threat, for the eyes closed again, the cat sighed and re-entered its rest.

There was a peg on the right side of the door, just above the latch, where a man entering the house would have a hard time missing it. Daav fetched the note out of his pocket and stood for a moment, holding it in his hand, head tipped, the back of his neck prickling.

He was, he was certain, being watched, and by something other than a cat.

"Yulie Shaper, good-day to you once more," he said, keeping his voice even. "Boss Korval thanks you for your care and accepts your offer. The note is here." He pressed the unfolded note gently over the peg. The paper broke and he slid it down until it seemed secure, absent a vigorous wind. He brought his hands to his sides, straining his senses, without, yet, turning around.

The watcher was behind him and to the right. He thought it might, indeed, be their skittish neighbor. If not. . .

Well, there was but one way to learn.

Daav turned on the step, keeping a careful eye out for the cat, which continued to drowse, as if all were as it should be. That was, he decided, comforting, and perhaps also a stroke in his favor. He looked out over the yard, carefully showing no *particular* interest in the large bush at the near right corner of the house.

"Boss Korval has asked me to walk the road between your land and ours, to determine what repairs may be needed," he told the yard pleasantly. "I will do my best to give you notice in advance of the arrival of work crews, so that you may gather the cats close in hand. The road work ought not to inconvenience you in any way."

He waited then, briefly, but their neighbor seemed to have nothing to bring to the conversation. That being so, he bowed slightly and went down the steps. The map in his head located the road directly in front of him, at the end of the gravel path leading to the house. He therefore walked down the path, scout-trained senses still registering a hidden observer, who nonetheless, and happily, seemed inclined to let him go.

The path curved slightly 'round a portly shrub, and there before him was the road.

Daav sighed, the sense of being watched departing altogether, and turned his face toward Jelaza Kazone.

THE ROAD HAD DWINDLED until it was scarcely as wide as a single small vehicle, narrowed further by grasping branches, above, and an encroaching gully, below. There were also large rocks situated inconveniently, and the occasional pothole.

Daav consulted the map he had memorized. Not very far now, to the house. He anticipated a hot shower—and perhaps his lifemate would deign to join him for a nap.

. . .whether his lifemate found this offer attractive, he could not say, as she remained outside his ken, occupied with whatever it was that occupied her when she was not manifest.

He had of course from time to time reflected upon Aelliana's state of existence. She had no substance of her own; no manifestation beyond a voice in his head. Occasionally, she claimed use of the body they co-habited—very seldom, really. Their adventures on the Clutch transport had improved her physical mastery; and he had expected, then, to find her more often in control of their route, yet she seemed content to be a passenger, observing their life through his eyes.

More than once, though not recently, he had asked her how she filled her time.

I fill my time as I have been accustomed to do. She'd answered his last inquiry with rather more tartness than he was accustomed to having from her; *with thought and with work.*

Which was all very well, but work wanted outlet, and thought the abrasion of other thoughts, to ignite insight. Locked inside his head, Aelliana had no opportunity to pursue her researches; she knew what he knew, though the conclusions she drew were often very different from his own. She had actively collaborated in the persona of Jen Sar Kiladi, as Kamele Waitley came to know him. Indeed, he had often thought that Kamele valued him most for those attributes which were peculiarly Aelliana.

Really, putting this road to rights was going to require not just the efforts of a grounds crew, but a forestry team, as well.

While they were rebuilding from the ground up, the delm might as well widen it, and straighten it, and possibly install a taxi-stand.

From behind him came the sound of a motor, accompanied by the occasional snap of a branch, and the crunch of gravel beneath wheels.

Daav stepped off the road and into a wide spot at the side, shouldering in among branches bearing hard, wrinkled berries, and last season's brittle thorns. He breathed out and reposed himself to silence.

The car came closer. It was, to Daav's ear, being driven with a respect for conditions that bespoke a pilot, or perhaps only someone who had dared to motor out this far before.

Eventually, it hove into view; largish, with a klaxon mounted on the roof. He glimpsed a dark face through the windscreen, then the vehicle was abreast of him, braking gently as the driver's window descended.

He took a breath, feeling himself come sharply alert, his senses open to all options, should the situation become. . .unfortunate.

The back door opened, and a tall man in pilot's leather stepped out onto the so-called road.

"Uncle Daav, what are doing here?"

He tipped his head, considering his nephew Shan gravely while still keeping half-an-eye or slightly more on the very dangerous person at the controls.

"I would say, waiting for a taxi, but I expect it will be some time before they are commonplace."

Shan smiled. "Maybe not as long as you think," he said walking forward.

A second person emerged from the back seat, a slender woman also in pilot leather, golden hair glimmering in the dull daylight.

"Nova," Daav said stepping softly out of the embrace of his thorn bush; "I am pleased to see you, child. Do I understand that this car contains all of Korval which is come in from the port?"

"Only Natesa, Shan, and myself," she said composedly. "The rest will come later, by whichever route suits them best." She moved her shoulders. "Pat Rin's house is busy enough, and we were becoming objects of interest. It seemed prudent, to come ahead."

"This," Shan continued, putting his hand over the track of the driver's window, "is Natesa, Pat Rin's lifemate. Natesa, this is our Uncle Daav. He makes a habit of skulking in the shrubbery, I fear."

Resignation and amusement reflected each other subtly in the driver's face.

"Good-day to you, Daav yos'Phelium. May I say that your son resembles you?"

"I would have said that he resembles his mother, but that is doubtless my own bias. It pleases me to make your acquaintance, Natesa, and I thank you for staying your hand."

She smiled. "You were in no danger from me, sir. Not only have I seen pictures, but just yesterday I had the pleasure of speaking with your son and his lifemate."

"Did you, indeed? I trust that they displayed their manners prettily, and were not the least bit of trouble to you."

This time she laughed. "They were everything that was gracious."

"It gratifies me to hear you say so."

"Uncle Daav," Nova said, interrupting this pleasant exchange. "May we give you a ride in the rest of the way? There's quite a lot of room in the back of this car."

"Thank you, but I believe that I must continue a-foot. Please do not hold yourselves back on my account. I do ask that the pilot," he bowed gently to Natesa, "continue her careful course. There are cats about which are connected to our neighbor's estate, and I have promised him that no harm will come to them through us."

"Yes," Natesa said composedly. "That provision is also in the contract."

"Ah, I had thought that Mr. Shaper was a man of sense! It is good to have my judgment vindicated." He stepped back off the road, and moved his hand, indicating that they should pass on.

"I'll walk with Uncle Daav," Shan said suddenly. "No slight to Natesa's driving, but I believe I could do with a little less lurching."

"Understood," said the driver, solemnly. "If it would not inconvenience those who come after, I might be tempted to abandon the car here and have us all walk in."

"And so you make the sacrifice for the greater good!" Shan gave her a grin, before turning to the rear of the car. Nova had already reentered, the door shutting behind her.

Shan raised a hand. "Until soon."

The car moved off.

"There is, you know, not the slightest need to stand my guard," Daav said, as they watched the dust sift through the chilly air. "I am quite capable of defending myself."

"I never doubted it. But, Uncle Daav, you make *such* a good excuse for getting out of that car!"

He laughed. "So that was candid, was it? Come along, then, but I'll warn you that this is no pleasure-walk."

"It isn't?" Shan considered him, slanted brows slightly raised. "Are we hunting rabbit?"

"Indeed we are not. The delm wished to have *eyeballs* on this road—an image I counsel you not to contemplate too closely—and saw no reason not to make one errand into two."

"That sounds like Miri." He looked around, shaking his head. "They call this *a road*?"

"That," Daav said, "also bears a remarkable similarity to Miri's remarks on the matter. I am to report on conditions, and present suggestions."

"The conditions are dreadful," Shan said, "and the solution is to bring in a work crew or six to widen, level, and fill. A little paving wouldn't go amiss, either."

"I agree," Daav said, stepping out on the road and taking up his stroll. "And you have given up your soft seat for nought."

Shan grinned and fell in beside him. "I need to stretch my legs."

"I wouldn't have thought that. What difficulty did Val Con and Miri occasion Natesa, I wonder?"

"For once, it wasn't their fault. Somebody noticed the Ring, knew it for Boss Conrad's and called security. Security called Natesa, who straightened it out in time for the two of them to get into the car and be introduced to the world." Shan paused, as if considering. "Pat Rin said that the trip out could have been more fraught."

"Poor children. But they, at least, seemed to have recovered their good humor with a night's rest. I trust that the same was true for their cousin."

"I'm don't think Pat Rin slept," Shan said. "What Nova said about his office not being half busy was an understatement."

"It would seem that he requires staff."

"Mr. pel'Tolian—Pat Rin's butler—came in with us. The last I saw him, he was directing a rather large and decidedly annoyed person to the *guest parlor*, with assurances that he would be called in his turn, and not one moment sooner."

"Excellent."

"It's a good start," Shan agreed.

They walked on for a few dozen paces in companionable silence, Daav noting a trace of mud in a gully that ran across the road, that might speak of a seasonal stream.

"I regret," Shan said, much more formally than he was wont, "that I missed meeting your daughter, my cousin, during her visit. Will she come to us again soon?"

Daav caught his breath against a twitch of pain, and kept his pace even.

"I believe that she must do so. There is unfinished business between herself and her brother."

There was a small pause.

"Uncle Daav," Shan said carefully, "are you quite well?"

Daav sighed. Shan was a Healer. To lie to a Healer was. . .difficult. Still, they were bound not to force themselves even upon those they considered to be in need, and they were, after all, merely human. Which meant that they could be distracted.

"I am a trifle tired, child," he said evenly, and turned his head to meet opaque silver eyes. "Our neighbor, the excellent Mr. Shaper, tells me that Boss Sherton undertakes to build a road to the sea. The delm was unsurprised."

"She must have been working on it for years," Shan said, obligingly following him into the new subject. "Considering what she has to work with and how far along it is. I'm going to propose to the delm that we offer to assist her—" He kicked at an embedded boulder, artfully missing—"since we'll be doing work of our own."

"That would," Daav said, "be neighborly, and a road to the sea must benefit all."

"It may benefit Korval more than most. I've been looking about Surebleak for a place to site yos'Galan's new house."

"Surely there's room at Jelaza Kazone for us all? And no need for a fortress to protect our valley, here. All we need do in order to remain inviolate is to fail to fix the road."

Shan grinned. "As you point out, it's hardly prudent for all of us to travel in the same car."

Daav inclined his head, acknowledging the point. "Yet, in terms of a strike from space, two houses as near as this location and the seacoast—"

"I have my eye on the archipelago that lies east and north of here."

"*North?*"

"Yes, it seems lunatic. However, according to Weatherman Brunner, once the mirrors are deployed in orbit, and tuned correctly, we should see some climatic benefit very quickly—and the situation I have in mind is only a few degrees nearer the pole." He sighed.

"The records of the founding company being what they are—or, more accurately, what they *aren't*—it becomes a challenge to know who, if anyone, may have a prior claim. Also, one would want to take a proper look around, and invite the scouts to do likewise. If they find the situation pleasing, then we might ease the pressure cooking of culture in the capital city."

"Do so many scouts follow the Dragon?" Daav asked, startled.

"Ms. dea'Gauss' database will be definitive, of course. My impression is that there is an. . .ideological divide between those who consider themselves to be scouts and those who consider themselves *Liaden* scouts."

"Yes, so Clonak had said. I had not understood the rift was so wide."

"Becoming wider, as I hear it—" Shan raised an arm to point. "*That* tree will have to come down, if we do nothing else."

"It is rather precarious, isn't it?"

"Speaking of precarious. . .Uncle Daav, *are* you well?"

Drat the child; he was as tenacious as his father had been.

He kept his voice cool. "As I had said, I am somewhat tired."

"I imagine that you would be, carrying Aunt Aelli all this while."

He sent a quelling glance into the boy's face.

"Does she weigh so much?"

"Who can tell the weight of a soul?" Shan mused, with the air of quoting something. "I wonder, too—forgive a nephew his natural concern for a favorite uncle!—if there might be another burden. One cannot help but see—"

"Can one not?" Daav interrupted, tartly. "I had thought Healers were given training."

"And so we are. However, having observed a certain flavor of melancholy, I can hardly *un*observe it, now can I?"

"I suppose not." Daav sighed, and turned his face aside, ostensibly scanning the edge of the track for other perilous trees.

Shan walked beside him, his patience almost tangible.

"If you will have it, the burden of my past necessities oppresses me this morning. Doubtless, the mood will pass."

The track curved; broken twigs littered the ground—a sign, perhaps of the car's recent passing. He looked ahead, where Surebleak's scraggly road, aided by a pair of planks, joined a wide, smooth drive, the sere plants and grudging weeds giving way to a plush blue-green grass. From ahead—and up—came a whine, growing steadily louder, and a flash above the tree.

Daav raised his hand to shield his eyes from the sullen sun, discerning the shape of a ship's shuttle.

"There," Shan said cheerfully. "That will be some more of us."

Author Commentary

HERE'S SOMETHING A little different—a couple of chapters that didn't make it into the final of *Ghost Ship*. They make a nice little scene, taken by themselves, and enhance the characters a bit. It was one of my regrets that, as *Ghost Ship* finally took shape, there wasn't any room for Yulie Shaper, Korval's new neighbor.

Enjoy!

Sharon Lee
September 21, 2011

Klamath Intro

An unfinished Liaden Universe® story cycle in Splinters
Introduction by Steve Miller

The story of Klamath is complex, and as we present it here in Splinter Universe, both unfinished and in disparate and at times conflicting pieces. Our parts in the story came from a piece of back-brain information that filtered through to us while *Agent of Change*, the first Liaden Universe novel, was in progress. That information was the news that Miri Robertson, mercenary soldier, had not always lived a pure and wholesome life and in fact had taken a bit of a detour from the straight and narrow following the the effective destruction of civilization on Klamath, if not before.

Understand that the Klamath story idea was a by-product of the originally sketched seven Liaden books; it seemed that there was information there we needed, but it didn't fit into the swell and swoop of the storyline. Still, in order to understand Miri, we nibbled around the edge of a Klamath novel over time, just as we made several quickly abandoned attempts to get into what many years later became the short *Crystal Soldier* sequence.

Processing that story through Miri was difficult; it seemed we needed more. More information, more backstory, more characters. Ichliad Brunner was added to the mix and became a fixture in our attempts to tell the story, but we couldn't overlook Skel, who'd also managed to creep into the main story line.

Stories *are* a process—and the process of writing the original three books in the Liaden saga was complicated by Real Life(tm) in the form of (boo! hiss!) work. The first book written but not yet sold, the household was moving on, and I took a series of retail jobs. It isn't that I was job-hopping per se, but rather that my skills fit easily into the "Retail Management" mold ... and I worked as an assistant manager of an expanding retail game (and computer) company that folded, got a job with a card and gift shop (moved to manager from part-time clerk) that folded and became assistant manager of another card shop which was on the way to being sold and staff downsized, had a management job with a kitchen and gift shop ..... .

The net result was that as the second and third Liaden novels (*Carpe Diem* and *Conflict of Honors*) were eventually written and sold, there was usually a Klamath floppy disk sitting around that I would pull out from time to time and ... extend. Or explore. Or fiddle with. This was one of those kitchen table stories I'd work on, bring to the table after dinner to discuss and amend over a glass of wine, and then put it back on the shelf for a week or a month or a year. The story was extended, cut back, brushed away, seen from several angles....but wasn't concentrated on and was often a stress reliever for me at a time when a sixty hour week was common and seventy hour week not unknown.

And then Sharon and I together got a chance to manage a storage facility. This let us work on the writing but by then we'd sold the first three books, two unwritten. Klamath was not one of the ones in the pre-sold pile.

By the time we moved to Maine, launched from the storage facility by a change in tax laws fatally removing our "free" house with the job, we'd fairly well got the seven mainline books in our head ... and Klamath, with starts and restarts and recursive bits and pieces, was archived in a bankers box for that move and then moved to the bottom and back of file drawers over time....

Still Ichhliad Brunner needed to be dealt with: he was, after all, someone that Miri owed. That story eventually came forward in a newly visualized way and was published at Jim Baen's Universe as the novella "Misfits".

And then, shoving things around to make room in the house for the relocation of the SRM Publisher office from Waterville following my hospitalization for pneumonia and cardiomyopathy, several of the Klamath splinters came to light once more. They got put into a pile—near the top of a pile!—and now that Splinter Universe is available, we figured we'd share with you what we have. Understand that the splinters may not mesh with each other; the timeline are inconsistent, the world goes through changes ... let's admit this as a *very rough* series of *rough* drafting. Still, there's stuff there—stuff we're unlikely to get back to in any other way in the next five years.

If you like the idea of seeing the rough drafts, you can send us support below, or from the splinters themselves, which I'll be posting over the next few weeks, one or two "chapter bites" at a time. Altogether they amount to somewhere between a quarter and a third of a novel. We'll be posting Mondays, around noon, for the most part.

Klamath

presented in Splinters
by
Sharon Lee and Steve Miller

1

No answer from the building. On the bluish lawn beneath the balcony lay assorted debris ejected during and apparently after the fight. Two chairs. Tape holders. Some kind of musical instrument resembling a bell with twin exhaust stacks. It was not yet dusk and the twin moons added strange highlights and multiple shadows. Commander Angela Lizardi called again.

"Sergeant Robertson, front and center!"

A bottle arced it's way lazily out of the broken window. Around Liz Lizardi the policemen scattered.

The bottle thumped on the lawn, refusing to break.

"Captain, may I borrow your loudtalker?"

The police captain who had fetched Lizardi to the altercation approached hastily, bearing the portable PA system.

"We don't know how dangerous she is, Commander. She threw all three of them out the window. She may be armed!"

"Give me that, Captain. I promise you, if she were armed and ready to fight you'd already have major casualties on your hands. Now let me talk, OK."

Lizardi pressed her lips in a straight line for a moment. If the whole thing weren't so grim to start with it would be funny, she knew. Just hijinks after an assignment, something to be paid off and laughed about down the road. Just blowing off steam. Just a binge. Sergeant Redhead versus the locals, part four.

Except that the binge was now several months old, and this was Miri.

"SERGEANT ROBERTSON. THIS IS YOUR COMMANDING OFFICER, COMMANDER LIZARDI. PRESENT YOURSELF FRONT AND CENTER. ON THE DOUBLE."

A crowd had begun to gather: they gasped as one as the red-haired figure flung itself onto and then over the balcony without hesitation, flipped in mid-air, and landed on its feet. The girl was bloody, and wobbly. She gathered her strength and marched directly for Lizardi.

"Sergeant Robertson reporting."

The salute was less than snappy, the voice slurred.

" Sergeant..."

"Sorry, " came the voice of the diminutive woman. "Sorry, Commander." Then she collapsed into a tiny, rag-doll pile on the blue lawn.

"LIZ, YOU DON'T UNDERSTAND. I didn't start the fight. Really, I didn't start it this time. That guy—the one I broke his nose. We'd been around together for a few days. Nothing special, but OK for a tumble or two, you know. Then in the middle of stuff he makes a com call and next thing I know he's got these friends of his wanting to wait in line."

"Liz, the worst thing is, they was gonna pay him! No by-your-leave or nothing. Just—that was it. I said no and I meant it, and the idiots wouldn't take the hint, guess they thought I was just some kind of stupid kid or something."

"Miri. I don't doubt they had it coming. If you were running your life by the Liaden code I'd guess we'd have a good cause for Balance against all of them. But you did it, too, girl. You were so gone you didn't see the problem till you had to hurt someone. You could have killed them all, throwing things around like that. You're lucky you're charged with Aggravated Assault and not Attempted Murder!"

"Lucky? Liz, what's wrong with you? Them..."

"Shut up Miri," came the voice, low. "Now."

Miri was silent, eyes big in her face. Liz stared at the girl a moment.

Miri"s long red hair, usually neatly braided, was stuffed into an ugly green headscarf. Her face was splotchy and purpled; her grey eyes seemed colorless amid the bruises.

"No more. Not even once more. I'll not come get you again, girl. They could have shot you, those police. You've got a history of violence here and they know you're a trained merc. They could have gassed the building. They could have brought in Thark-hounds and I'd have been having to bury pieces. I've lost too many, Miri. I can't live the rest of my life rescuing you and I can't wake up each day wondering if I have to spend it watching you be sick again from whatever you've been on for the last however many months. You have to get on with things, like all of us do. Got it?"

"Liz, you ain't leaving me here like this?" The girl gestured around her, hands taking in the bed in the cell-like room.

"I can if I have to. Listen to me, hear? I'll drop you from the unit if I need to, but I don't want to. If you tell me you want to get over this, fine. I'll do whatever's in my power. If you want to go on as you are I'll tell the man out there you've resigned from Lizardi's Lunatics and you can fight it through by yourself. Got it?"

"Liz, you're always here. You got me away for Surebleak and ..."

"It doesn't look like I have, Miri. I'm going to walk around the grounds once. When I come back in you'll tell me yes or no. I'll pull with you–all of us we got left will pull–with you!–if you want to get things right. Otherwise they'll deport you back to Surebleak on your bill."

The Commander gathered herself together, nodded to Miri, and nodded to the guards at the door on her way out.

2

MY NAME IS SERGEANT Miri Robertson of Lizardi's Lunatics. I've been a Lunatic for almost seven Standards, and that feels like most of my life. I'm 19 Standards old and I was born on Surebleak, which doesn't count for much. I have a hard time right now concentrating.

The light isn't so good and the keyboard they have in here is built into the desk so I can't hurt myself. That means I can't adjust it so good though, because this place is built for Terrans and I'm smaller than most Terrans. Back on Surebleak they say I'm mutated within acceptable limits. That don't count much on Surebleak because they don't much care. I think the only reason they do the test is because the have to for the trade rules or something.

I've been here two days so far. Liz got me moved out of that jail hospital by promising to have me treated. The only thing wrong with me is Klamath, I bet. I've been a bit wild since then, but there's a lot that needs forgetting. Haven't had anything much to eat or drink except a lot of greens and brown bread and water.

It's OK, I guess. Not much to do, though. It reminds me of being on ship waiting for drop onto someplace except I don't have all much to study or read. Guess I miss the Lunatics ...wish I had some kynak or something. There's not many Lunatics left. I don't really know how long I've been here—they took my watch. The screen prompt has a number that changes and think it's hours and days. I don't know what day it is, though because I lost track a bit there before Liz brought me over. Damn.

This place has no windows and the door won't open to my palm. I wonder if they keyed it against me because it seems to open for everyone else OK. If I get bored I'll try my foot.

There's been a couple of people in to see me. Some guy, doctor of something or other, gave me a physical and a few word association things that don't prove much if you're not from here. I think they thought I was a kid until my unit records came.

I wish Liz would have told me, though–I peeked a look at the records and they said that Lizardi's Lunatics were currently "inactive"–she's not hiring no one. I think what I really need is a chance to go fight an honest war. All I want is a planet that sits still under your feet and a place where the wind... ah damn, complaining again. I'd like to forget that place. Except for Skel's there, and Joey, and all that it ain't a very important kind of place. Never was. Not even worth fighting a war about. Oh yeah. Some woman came in ask me if I wanted to prefer counter-charges against those guys. Three to one – I can't prove a thing 'cause this place don't allow truth tests. Hmmph. They all know what they was doing.

Should have broke more than his damn nose and a leg and a rib or two. "Circumstances" they want to call it. Due to circumstance Sergeant Miri Robertson will be remanded to the custody of her Superior Officer and a certified treatment center." Circumstances. They going to pity us all because we was on Klamath? Damn. Wonder if there's alcohol in the mouthwash.

Guess not, eh, this being a place to get someone clean? No drugs, no kynak, no fun. Gets tiring staring at the walls all day, and I ain't going to watch the damned therapy videos this place shows. I ain't crazy. Just a soldier needs something to do. Tired of staring at the wall. Just plain tired. I could use some Cloud real bad. Real bad! Tired and jittery, sleepy and wired...don't make so much sense.

Cloud. Cloud'd help more than kynak cause kynak reminds me of Skel sometimes. Cloud just lets me be here now. Here now hear now hear this...

I'll sleep under the damn bed when I get tired. I'm little enough to do it, and it'll give 'em a freak for a minute. Might be able to get out that way if i need to . . . Hide and sneak out. Might work. Might be some Cloud out there.

3

"SHE'S GOT DEMON SPEED, Commander, as you probably know. What you don't know is how desperate she is right now. It's been five days since she had any buffering drugs at all, including alcohol. We've been sending her food in via the rotator even though we like to keep some kind of human presence when possible. She very nearly faked the door into letting her out by using her foot; luckily our technician spotted her on the monitor and overrode the controls or it might have worked."

Angela Lizardi nodded. Miri was bright and she'd try to find a way out. Any way out. The Commander had had addicted soldiers before and had tried to see them all through it. That is, when they'd wanted help. They got mean, they got smart, they got cruel. Sometimes, they got better.

The problem was that the other soldiers had not been Miri, the only child of her own childhood friend. Nor had the other soldiers been so damn good at being a soldier as Miri could be. And so Liz sat in this tiny cubicle of an office, drinking local spring water out of a fragile paper cup while Miri was locked in nearby. Locked in by Liz's own orders.

"And so we've been pretty well reduced to hand foods right now, since she sharpened the plastic edge of the cup on something and by folding it a few times managed to make a pretty effective blade. She can only get her water from the fountain right now. I'm afraid she hasn't hit the worst of it yet, since she'd been able to keep at the keyboard for as long as two hours at a time."

"She's tough." Liz said to the therapist. "How long once she gets-to the zero point?"

The woman shook her head.

"That's really hard to tell. She was in good shape physically when she came in, but the blood serum levels of the stuff were almost as high as someone who'd been taking it for a couple of years. Mostly the addicts we get in here aren't in shape at all—they're kind of worn out already.

Liz nodded again. Maybe they didn't understand.

"She grew up on Surebleak. It killed her mother early. Nearly killed her a dozen times, I guess. Thing is that she knows how to live on practically nothing– spent years living that way. Her weakness is she likes pretty things and thinks she don't deserve them. Pretty people, good times: admires them all but doesn't expect them. This is just another tough time."

The therapist pointed to computer screen. "Do you see what she was taking? Did you know?"

"I didn't follow my troops around to make sure they were being good little..."

"Then what you need to know is on this screen. She was on a mixture of things when you brought her in. Alcohol was one, and a local inhalant called tristan-root. They masked the big problem for awhile, which was Cloud. It acts to short circuit long-term memory–anything up to a day or two is clear, and the farther back you go the less clear you get. I understand it's possible to be selective: you can tell yourself when you take it that you don't want to remember thus-and-so. That's the reason it's dangerous, too, because people forget that memory has a lot of triggers. So something comes up that reminds them of what they didn't want to recall and they take a little more Cloud."

Liz stared at the screen: graphs showing danger levels of the drugs and the time for each to zero out in Miri's system.

"So Cloud has built up to amazing levels in your soldier. When she hits zero point—when the last of the accumulated Lethecronaxion goes back into solution and stops inhibiting those memory paths—that's the bad time. It's as if the inhibition acts as an irritant and once it's gone the way to scratch the itch is to remember again. Hard, fast, and frequently."

Lizardi hardly noticed the water in her hands as she involuntarily crushed the cup.

"How long?" she managed to ask.

"It will start sometime today. It could last a week, or even more. Some just never come out of it at all."

"Let me know when it starts. I'll be if available whenever. If I can help, page me through the Hiring Hall."

"There's really not much more you can do."

"I took her to Klamath, Doctor. I brought her back here alive. She's damn well going to live a real life. Got it?"

"It's up to her, Commander. It's up to her now."

6

KLAMATH. THE THIRD world of the five planet system designated A770-00-412XX in the Kammerman Catalog of Rated Star Systems. The system is stable, though young, and the star itself – named Grauss 14th after the first Terran visitor to the system – is typical of stars attractive to human colonists. It has a long-duration oscillation resulting in a well defined solar wind but also has an extremely complex series of mildoscillations resulting in a highly variable magnetic complex that extends outward to the fifth and largest planet, Grausbet. Grausbet, at nearly .223 the mass of the primary, also generates a powerful magnetic field due to its own high rate of rotation.

Klamath is a young, active volcanic world in the midst of geologic and meteorologic transitions. As such it was declared "Offlimits" by a Terran survey group, "Lazenia do'trant" by Liaden Scouts, and was considered technically uninhabitable until the Emilthurnian revolution resulted in fully 3.5 million of the survivors being exiled there starting in Standard 779. Despite the protests of Survey and Scouts after the fact, the planet has remained inhabited since that point. A combined Liaden, Federation, and Terran mission remains in orbit around Klamath to observe the rather striking meteorologic and geologic conditions as they unfold.

The eccentric meteorological conditions include three sets of highly variable jet streams which tend to meander ... damn well do meander ...all over the place everyday ...

You gotta toast 'em when you say their names! Never did get past V, I bet. Does Liz know what you're doing to me? Maybe the cleaning crew missed something–I better check!

THE BLACK PENNANT SNAPPED jauntily as Miri quick-marched the unit from the shuttle. The pennon was all they were allowed until the local flags came to head them up: they were to expect them in a few hours. In the meantime the large buff crescent with its two smaller followers smiled over them as Miri counted 100 paces in a straight line, called a right-ho, marched them 200 more and then called a stand-to with a salute to the shuttle.

The parade stuff was OK: they were the third group of mercs down this morning and the locals had arranged a friendly drop. Somewhere on the hill to the north was the True Reader who'd hired them; Miri hoped he was impressed.

Several jet craft prowled a distant perimeter and another shuttle was due down. Miri watched the shadows move across the landing ground: thick clouds that cut off the sunlight in a hurry, wispy clouds that let a dingy light through for a moment or two and then evaporated, and then bright again. The wind shook them lightly from all directions at once as the Laughing Man danced about on his flagstaff.

Miri liked the smell. She could smell dirt, and it smelled clean; she could smell water – the several streams north and west of the field she'd seen on the monitor as they were landing, no doubt–and it, too smelled clean.

The last of the Lunatics were clear.

"Robertson, give me an about and a quick one thousand. As you arrive start us a quick wall: we want to look organized before the Jackals come in. Go."

"Gotcha." Miri spoke back to the voice from her helmet. "Going."

"Up and one-eighty, quickmarch. Joey give me count of one thousand. First three rows have your trenchers unlimbered before we get there. I want the Laughing Man on a double pole before we stop. Let's go on ten. And oh yeah, I got a whole bottle of kynak for the first of my unit to see and report a hostile! Got it? Heyup! Eight nine TEN!"

That fast they were moving. No time to sight see, no time to wonder if this world was really worth fighting about, no time to watch Shuttle C gather itself slowly from the field and leave them all behind.

As they marched the shuttle rose, cast its shadow over them and finally sauntered into the low clouds precisely on their heading. One of the local jets tried to tag along, but it was no match for even so ordinary a spacecraft.

. . .

Where was I? Oh. . .right.

The atmosphere of Klamath is nearly .05 richer in total oxygen than Terra and hence about .055 richer than Liad and most of the Liaden or Terran colonies. *The high ... hell. Wait minute. Missed something here.*

Oh yeah. Something about the mountains. No, it was something about the poles. I'll remember it yet...

You can't beat me, you know. I stopped shaking long enough to get this on screen, and I still want a drink. I still want my Cloud. You think you're going to make me remember it all, but I can keep busy with this stuff forever. You got that?

Geologic evidence collected by Terran Survey 7198/A14 indicates that the Klamathian internal magnetic field has flip-flopped as recently as Standard 564, and before that as recently as Standard -012. Liaden evidence indicates the possibility of an intermediate flux not in evidence in the Terran survey region.

See? When I really think about something I'm not stupid. Not stupid. They wouldn't have made me Sergeant if I was stupid. Bad luck it had to be Klamath, that's all. No one should have gone to that place. But you can't make me remember them, damn you. I read lots and lots of stuff and you can have all of it ... every damn word I can remember. I don't have to tell you about Skel, though ...

Hell. Just give me a drink, just some kynak. Mentioned his name. Gotta toast 'em, you hear me? Give me some kynak or even some of that local ale...

"SARGE, THERE'S A STORM coming!"

Miri was instantly awake. "Shiu. It's been raining off and on half the night ..."

"Quick ,Sarge, you better come!"

Miri rolled out of the sleep sack, listening to the noises of the night. The wind noises she identified easily, like the keening of the high-tensioned plastic of the tarp-tent. Rain, big drops of it, struck her face as she started out into the night.

"This better be good... Oh, no!"

"See what I mean? I didn't know what to do and ..."

"Get em all up, now. Hurry it up, Shiu. Give 'em a yellow alert whistle." It took but a moment for Miri to touch a stud at her belt.

"All units of Lunatics. Alert yellow, alert yellow. Heads up in a hurry. Please advise Commander Lizardi instantly,"

"Liz here, Miri" came the half-asleep voice. "Hostiles?"

"Liz, take a look out. It'll hit us first, but it's – damn. It's, Liz, it's like weather like I never saw."

"Miri, I hope you ... FULL ALERT! FULL ALERT! Heathrow call the other mercs! Miri, just hang on and keep us in touch; suggest you hit the trenches!"

All of Miri's unit were awake and out, all staring at the same menace.

It appeared as a column, dark dark dark at the base and rising to a weird greenish glow at the top, fraught with bright flashes. It was bearing down on them rapidly. As they stood transfixed the sound of it began to beat at them: roar with the sound of thunder reaching out subtly at first and then with increasing power.

The sheer immensity of it!

Miri looked around her, brought back to the moment by the sound of a mumbled prayer to the Goddess asking that Balance be brought slowly....

"Trench it everyone, set up for rain. Everything that's not staked down I want in the trench with us. Give me a big hole – you got twenty seconds! Throw anything in you can reach. Go!"

An explosion then, resounding for a moment and then torn away as the wind picked up the sound and smothered it. Into the new crater streamed Miri's unit, carrying bundles and boxes, towing larger equipment on the skids. As if they'd practiced this a hundred times before, they went in once, each with something, came back out to dive into the trench as the greenish light spread among them with a mind-numbing wrench.

Water battered at them as a thunderous breaker; at them trying to pluck them from their precarious dugout. In a moment they were standing ankle deep in the cold, frothing water. A second wave of sound struck, this one a constant head-splitting roar. Miri yelled into the communit, heard not even the echo of her own voice in her ear unit, felt only the cold rushing at her with the blown liquid wave. Through barely slitted eyes the green fire leapt at her: lightning originating within feet of her, slamming the ground with a dance and then dashing away to catch up with the storm front. The madness went on; Miri grabbing a hand that came near her and holding on for sheer sanity of knowing that she was not totally alone in it all. The water was nearing her knees now and the roar settled into separate bursts of thunder. Without warning the rain stopped: with it the roar diminished so fiercely that the apparent silence itself was a blow to the body.

"Count off! Count off! One!" Miri screamed into the communit, and hearing the count start and go on she switched to the master channel.

"Hold hands, get equipment secure and then hold hands till it goes by. PIease! And oh no!"

The roar came back, with Miri still trying to scream into the communit, knowing that she couldn't hear her own voice. How long was it going to last? She was blasted by the rain and what? A rock?

Ice! Chunks of ice the size of her fist were falling on them now. Miri found she'd let go of the arm she'd had, called out "There, someone, get them all to lean into the earth, this way, pass it on, lean into it and the ice can't get as much of you, please understand!"

The ice whipped at them ceaselessly. The combat vests and hats shielded some of their number, but Miri knew injuries, maybe deaths would result from this horrendous beating.

Thunder, individual peals of thunder! wind noticeably: the greenish light was by them, gone. They were still whipped with something from the sky, but now it was snow. SNOW!

Large chunky flakes of it clung to Miri, found ways to cover her goggles, to throw itself into the water they were still standing in. Thunder came less frequently, like an afterthought.

"Recount! Count off!" Miri heard the voice on the communit, realized she'd been screaming it into the wind since the roar'd come back.

"One," sounded out," two, three," an empty three beat pause, "five!" and Miri lifted her hand to wipe the snow from her goggles and her face. " Where"s Shiu? Who has seen Shiu?"

"Four dammit, four four four four friggin' four, OK? Shiu's got the mic out of the water, OK?"

"Gotcha, seven? Lets keep it going, gang, give me a count and get your feet out of this stuff. "

The landscape was alien now: streams of water flowing down the hills and through the whitness of soggy snow, coming down with a silent violence of its own. The wan light was scattered by the night. Miri could see nothing of other units.

"Lunatics? Lunatics?" she called into the communit. The scanning receiver brought back strange echoes, and her ears were filled again with the roar of the rain – this time from some other unit where the snow had not yet ...

"Report One, Unit One reporting." Corporal Shiu stood in front of Miri, recognizable in the snow by the tilt of her hat and her height. In hand sequence she filled Miri in as Miri spoke into the communit.

"One here. We have three missing right now. Search is underway. There's a couple of broken bones. All our heavy stuff is either underwater or under the snow somewhere, but we can mount a patrol in about two minutes as I talk. We already have four – no five guards up. Injuries – one's found. It's Witzinak, crushed leg. He's been given knock outs ... l swear it looks like a block of ice fell on him ..we've got radio all around now: one still missing, heavy snow."

The snow had evened out to allow an easy seventy paces or so of visibility.

"One Report out, I've got to mount some patrols! "

"Gotcha one, our recontact is in fifteen. Mark!"

Miri touched her watch in it's case, set the timer.

"Joey! Infrared all around, and get me some touch grids too!"

"Got grids laid east, give me a minute to find the damn ... you'll have it, Sarge!"

"Right. Quick, Joey, talk to me about headcounts and casualties."

Damn, damn, dammit, did I say Joey again? Did I say Joey again? Need some kynak – way it's s'posed to be. Give me my kynak if you won't let me forget, damn you all!

7

"COMMANDER? MAY I SPEAK with you?"

"Of course , Doctor. My time is yours."

"Thank you, Commander. The subject is somewhat delicate. You may wish to step into my office..."

"As you wish, Doctor."

The hall echoed with his steps. Hers were silent, and had she been alone the only sound at all would have been that of the air moving in the air events, and the occasional click made by a light tube cycled off or on by the housekeeping computer.

The office was modest; the seat Liz Lizardi sat in well used but comfortable. The doctor sat, fumbled with some odds and ends on his desk top, finally punched up the computer as he began to speak. "Commander, it grieves me to ask this, but we must keep all aspects of treatment in view."

"Prudent," she granted him.

"Ah. Well, What we need to do, I"m afraid, is to be sure that financial considerations won't force us to discontinue... "

"My money is good, Doctor."

"Yes. Well. Let us hope so. Are you aware of this problem?"

Liz Lizzardi glanced at the screen: daily news.

In a moment she started cursing quite colorfully in several languages, none of which the doctor was fluent in. Finally she spoke in Trade.

" I can't see why anyone wants to freeze the assets of the units that fought on Klamath. Stupid. Still, they name three outfits, none of them mine. One of them, the only survivor is a corporal. Lucky so-and-so, too. So they want to freeze assets until they figure out what happens to him. What can I do for you?"

"What we need, I'm afraid, is something more than your verbal assurance that—as you say—your money is good. The news says that some of the units did not get paid for their work on Klamath—that they were robbed, or hoodwinked. I'm afraid I'll have to ask ....

"Doctor, don't bother me with this. All you have to do is check with my insurance company. I'll tap it out for you now if you wish." Before he could say no she'd cleared the screen and tapped out a code, then another. In a moment the screen reformatted.

She turned the screen with a deft flip of her wrist.

"There's my local account info. Fresh update, today. If you check with their office yourself you"ll find they're on twenty-two planets—it's why we chose 'em. Got that? I want you to use your head, too. I carry insurance for up to seven hundred soldiers and support. I got about hundred who're retired but are still covered. Coverage reads that active duty coverage may be transferred on muster out or death. Right now, doctor, beside my hundred odd retired, I got six survivors on the damn active list. Plus, in case that"s not enough coverage, you can always put a lien on Miri's retirement pay if you want. I filled out all your applications for Miri with my name, too. You got my assets if you need them, personal assets. Now tell me you think Miri'll run through a thousand cantra worth of health insurance here."

"I'm sorry Commander, I didn't mean to... "

"Look–you make her well. I got too many things to be mad about to be mad about you. I'll be in the lounge if you need me."

And she was gone from the little office, leaving no noise behind her.

The doctor was suddenly struck by the thought that maybe it wasn't too good an idea to rile up one of Klamath's survivors. After all, Robertson was one of those survivors and it had taken half a police department to collect her, tiny as she was, when she was three days drunk and filled with Cloud. Imagine what her commander could do cold sober and with malice?

Not comforted, he checked the info on the screen and had it transferred to his data banks. It suddenly didn't seem likely at all that the assets of Lizardi's Lunatics would be bothered.

"Forgive me, Commander, if I intrude an an awkward moment."

The Commander had been watching the door, as if waiting, when she entered. A moment's grimace, followed by appraisal.

"Every moment I'm here's an awkward moment. You a Healer? I know someone that could use a Healer, if I thought I could trust you."

"Alas, I am not a Healer. Instead I am a Corresponding Attorney."

"You are Liaden, aren't you?"

"Yes."

"If you're here to tie up my assets, forget it. Untouchable."

"No, I am not here for your assets. I am here to speak to you of your employee Miri Robertson."

"Goddess, help me. What else did she do?"

"That is what I am here to find out. If I may sit and explain my needs?"

"Sure. Yes. Why not?"

"Thank you. I am here on the behalf of a Liaden citizen. . .one who apparently knew Miri Robertson on Klamath."

Liz shook her head instantly.

"Must be the wrong person, unless Miri snuck out that first night. . .that was when that first storm hit us. I'd say 'no,' not much of a chance."

"Please let me continue."

The woman was nearly as short as Miri, and her voice was well trained and soft. Liz nodded in her direction, then caught herself and bowed a bow of assent.

"I represent Ichliad Brunner, a Liaden citizen attempting to regain access to various estates belonging to his family. The *melant'i* of the situation is quite complex because. . ."

"I missed a word there. You also have not identified yourself. I am Commander Lizardi. You know this. You are?"

It was the young woman's turn to bow. " I am Terlisa yos'Denali. I am a Corresponding Attorney for the firm of Solcintra Realty and Property Trusts, AKG, attempting to help settle several estates. We find however that Ichliad Brunner is detained for infringements of local and Liaden law and custom while in service on the station circling Klamath as ...."

"The weatherman, right? I couldn't place the name at first. He was the meteorologist on the station!"

"Yes," said Terlisa yos'Denali. "Exactly. The weatherman."

"LOOKS TOO DAMN MUCH like home, Shiu, I could have lived my life and been happy not see nothing like this again."

Miri's supposed vantage point looked out over a field covered in mushy snow, over which lay a nearly impenetrable fog. The light reached them in dim grayish tones, shadowless. The only color at all was the bright pinpricks of the sensor displays: reds, ambers, blues, and bright whites that drew the eye.

"Joey?" Miri said into the fog.

"Gotcha."

"What's it look like? Any signs of motion?"

"Sure, Miri. Movement in the Lunatics behind us. . .guess they're still looking for the missing over in the next unit. And the guys from Alexanders Legions are still wandering in and out of their camp like no one's in charge. It's a good thing we haven't got hostiles out there."

"Yeah, Joey. Let me know if anyone comes close at all, Lunatics or Legion. And put your displays on low output, huh? You glow so bright I'm surprised Liz ain't complaining."

"Gotcha, Sarge."

The single casualty had been hit by a block of ice: they'd stumbled on it while looking for the missing. The missing, it turned out, turned out, suffered from equipment damaged by the ice-fall; all three had been found, though Grelph, stuck under a fallen box in the crater, had come within a few inches of drowning in the downpour.

8

"THERE YOU ARE, BRUNNER!"

The voice startled Geophysicist Class One Ichliad Brunner; in that second of astonishment several of the fragile spikes of mineral in his hand crumbled and the specimen slipped from his grasp.

Brunner caught it without thinking, grimaced at the sudden pain. There was blood in his hand now, blood and several odd looking pebbles mixed with foamy sand.

"Yes, in fact, Manager, I am. Or was. I've cut myself on the sample and don't have time to speak with you now."

That quickly the manager was left behind. Despite the pain and anger Brunner moved gracefullydown the hall way and into the small medcenter.

"Got a cut or two," he told the lounging medtech, "from a sample I picked up yesterday."

"Dirtside sample?" the Terran asked lazily from his seat.

"Yes. Mineral sample, with inclusions."

"I guess we ought to take a look , eh?"

Brunner looked down again, realizing that he still clutched the blue-qray remains in his hand.

It was an odd sight to him: his blood mixed with powdered rock from the strange planet below. Powdered rock and pebbles that had taken thousands of years to grow into a fragile crystal and a half-second of clumsiness to crush.

He dropped the sample onto the table top and washed his hand in the sink indicated by the tech. In a moment the hand was immobilized inside an autodoc sleeve, in a moment more the tech's screen lit up with a mix of trade and Terran symbols.

"Mostly aluminum and related compounds, nothing overtoxic in the current ratios. Wouldn't want to eat the stuff, though. Hold still a second."

The "second" was a little longer than that and Brunner felt the tension rising in him.

"Hey – I told you there isn't anything to worry about, didn't I?"

"Yes." Brunner looked at the screen, embarrassed momentarily as he watched several indicators rise: pulse and blood pressure.

He gasped at the sight, the tension rising in him, took a deep breath. A friend had taught him to realx, long ago, and he tried to recall the method...

He concentrated on the placement of his feet, on paradoxically relaxing his shoulders so he could stand straighter. The tension dropped out of him and the telltale lines fell on the screen.

The autodoc hummed burped pleasantly, and sprayed his hand with a light bandage.

"That'll come off in about twelve hours or so. You'll have some new pink skin. That'll look normal in about two days.

"What is this stuff?"

Brunner shrugged, a habit he deplored in himself.

"A crystal growth of sorts. A rock. A work of art, it was ... Sharp, also. Fragile. I called it Sapphire Lace."

"Pretty. Sounds odd to me. But that's not your specialty is it? Rocks, I mean?"

"No, it is my interest, my ... hobby, you would have it. I work here on weather patterns."

The man nodded, turned his back to Brunner, closed drawers.

"Weather. This is a great place to watch. . .I've never seen a place where you can see storms move so quick from this far away. Pretty, too, if you like staring at something for awhile and just watch colors change. I saw that red storm down south yesterday, made the place look like it was glowing. Went real good with my meal and a good strong drink."

Brunner smiled briefly, a social smile unseen by the medtech. It didn't matter. It didn't really matter.

BRUNNER SLID HIS DOOR closed behind, glad to hear the slight change in the air system as he did so. His small world was adjusting to his presence.

He liked the full four percent decrease he could achieve without special dispensation. The Manager complained that it made his job harder: that was hardly Brunner's concern.

SPLINTER UNIVERSE PRESENTS!

The Manager. Damn the Manager! And what concern was it of the Manager what Brunner did? Brunner belonged to the Geophysical Task Force. His duty was to the collecting and interpreting of information on the strange planet below. The Manager managed only the station itself: the physical structure and its workings were his concern. Grenda yos'Dala was Brunner's true superior, as was the quietly mad Jocon ter'Minthen. The Manager? A fool, dumb to the universe, reading the all of existence as a matter of some savant's declaration of an ideal and perfect air pressure.

He shook his hand, caught himself before he banged it into the bed. Still with the sudden rage on him he picked up his flat pillow and threw it to the floor, kicked it, cursed briefly in a language he hardly knew. The Manager should be dismissed. For that matter ter Menthen herself should be dismissed. Perhaps he, Brunner, should be dismissed. The world they were studying could hardly care about them. Why should they care about it?

Even as he thought that Brunner caught his rage and wrapped it around a rumor. The rumor was that a Scout would be coming ahead of schedule. If that was so, perhaps the Manager could be removed.

Maybe some good changes could occur.

Brunner's eyes focused on the chart he'd clamped to his wall the first day he'd arrived on Klamath Station S. Two Standards and most of another had gone by since then; and except for the occasional jab of the Manager or some other petty politician they had been a good, nearly a happy time for Brunner.

The chart a standard planetary flow chart for a planet the size of Klamath, at the distance Klamath was from it's primary,and with the density and mass distribution originally charted for Klamath.

Below it was a single hand-sketched view of the planet. Klamath couldn't exist as it did, said the chart. The sketch was Brunner's own, his very first effort at understanding the planet he orbited now. He was glad it did exist: he needed something to understand. He needed it very much.

9

BRUNNER NEARLY FELL over Trina as he made the turn into the weather room. She was backing out and he was looking more at the packages in his hands than at anything else.

"Hmph. . .hello. Pardons, please. I didn't see you. . ."

"Yes, and I also didn't see you. Fewer things are your fault than you would have the world believe, Ichliad."

"That we will not discuss. I will tell you I was looking at the packages. . .data tapes from the surface."

"And not expecting me to be approaching best side forward!"

"Yes. How would I expect that? It has not been so easy to see you for awhile."

"You have seen far more of me in the last few days than you have in the rest of our time here," she chided gently, "and I do not suggest its all my idea. Yet I was looking for you. I thought I might debrief you."

"I don't have the information yet. It's here."

He tapped the packages.

"Would you like to watch?"

She bowed a careful bow, then smiled.

"ITS TRUE ABOUT LIADENS...they can have your heart's desire, but if you don't ask, they won't *tell* you. Besides, we need other information not in the packages. Tell me about the people you spoke with..."

He did so as they entered the workroom, going as far as to tell her of the difficulty with *melant'i* he'd encountered with the woman.

"It is unfortunate," Ichliad Brunner was saying, "that we haven't been able to calibrate the equipment being used. I understand that it is of good quality. Yet if we *knew* that the five different units read within the same half percent it would help."

Trina was watching the weather simulation screen with some interest, letting the topic of the people go for the moment. Brunner hardly noticed: his vocation was upon him like a shadow.

On the screen was the weather at Point 478 as they had recorded it.

"Look. Here was our projection, and here. . ." he said, touching a switch, "is what happened over the next three hours or so."

The projection, in blues and greens, went one way slowly, while the actual weather system picked up speed, moving ever more rapidly in another direction.

"Now. Here is with the local conditions added in."

The simulation of the actual weather showed more detail: the clouds were thicker it seemed in one section, and there was clear spot elsewhere that hadn't been in the first simulation.

"This is the projection with the rest of this data—and the data I got from your report of yesterday—added in."

For a few moments the two images were as one. Then a slow, sidewise drift seemed to hit the projection and it pivoted its way around a mountain side.

"Can you study the difference between the prediction and the reality?" Trina asked.

"It is done daily," he said tonelessly as he watched the screen.

"Yes. Of course. I didn't mean..."

"Forgotten. Tell me what you see, please?"

"It looks like the projection was off because of a wind or something, like it got blown off course..."

"Yes!" he agreed with animation. "Wrong question answered."

"I see." She paused for a moment and then continued. "Is it required?"

"To use resources best, yes. This current information base will change randomly?"

"Not random."

Neither spoke for a moment: on the screen Brunner set up another simulation.

Finally: "Not random, Ichliad. Either a wise command or a weak plan by the Domain of Inch. Perhaps both. The groups are getting accustomed to the weather problems. They are learning to cope. None of them is in an attack position, though these three spots here: she pointed to the simulation currently on the screen, might be advance bases for a local march."

He nodded as he fiddled with controls a moment more. Then, turning to look at her carefully, he said a word in Terran.

"But?"

"Just guessing, my friend? Ah, Liadens...yes. But. But. *But* I don't think they will march. I think this is designed draw attention while arrangements are made. I don't think it wise to attack a border area with the entire countryside not yet mobilized. I expect a strike at any of a dozen targets. You may well have sensors stretching from the Domain all the way across the sea and into the northern cap. "

"I can arrange daily contact. Direct contact. This will help me predict the weather. Will it help you?" This was said quietly, and without inflection.

We cannot be seen as allies of either side, my friend," said Trina.

"I will have my information, Trina. It is closer to me now than before. Who knows where a key is to be found?"

"Who indeed? I cannot stop you from cooperating with anyone who offers information. It may even be necessary. I too want the information. A puzzle to solve. . .a truth, maybe."

She watched the screen as the weather prediction churned on, running by program and now bearing little relationship to any of the real events...

"You will send information then? As well as receive it?"

"How else? Twice daily, an update on a general band; four times daily, updates on five areas—they have five units capable of the required measurements and broadcasting—and as required, but no more than a dozen per day, mind, for one unit."

He was silent a moment now as he copied the information in the files for her.

"Why only one, Ichliad?"

"I am not staffed to predict for a war. We already do hourlys automatically to four tightcast locations...more than that—two for each side—and I don't think we will be considered either neutral or desirable. So, one field unit, We'll call this a third side."

Trina said nothing for a moment, watching the storm sequence on the screen to flow off the edge of the field of vision, as if it now dripped onto the floor.

"I'll be able to give you some intercepts as well. That is good."

"So it will be then. I will tell the Commander Lizardi that it shall be one of her units. The one with the Liaden handling the equipment."

Trina laughed quietly.

"Right. I didn't realize your joke, my friend. Three sides to anything...the right side, the wrong side, and the Liaden side."

"If a choice needs be made, it should satisfy someone. This choice satisfies me."

She bowed.

"Of course. I would consider favorably sharing some time later, my friend. I must go."

He bowed back. A bow with implicit request.

"I would like that very much. Better,too, if we might wake up together."

"I also. Perhaps the bell will be silent tonight."

10

"ANOTHER PROBLEM SOLVED" Miri said out loud as she saw the arriving replacements. Paulia was among them, as was the fickle Donnee.

"What's that Sarge?"

"Nothing Joey. . .nothing at all. Just noticing that we have local transport this time."

"Yeah. Great, huh?"

"Sure. Least it's not horses."

Joey didn't answer that one as the noisy trucks pulled up to the pennant pole where Miri waited.

"Look! It's *Skel*!" Joey called out. "How'd he get here?"

It *was* Skel, and he was, in a manner of speaking, driving one of the odd vehicles.

"End of the line" he yelled out at the top of his voice, "unless you got round trip fares,"

Miri found herself grinning.

It was Skel all right! It really was.

"...AND SO IT WAS THAT I found out that that Aus guy was shipping out, and I knew that the Lunatics were gone already, and so I kinda got myself a personal service contract with Rolf. Told him that if we got where he was going and the Lunatics weren't there I'd just regular up with him for the action..."

Skel stopped a moment now, fighting the strange needs of the vehicle. The transmission was totally mechanical, as were all of the controls. The machine didn't like climbing hills. It didn't like going down them or up them.

Actually it seemed best suited to sitting still, thought Miri. She was sore from the one way trip and wondered how well the guards and drivers had come through the so far on the round-trip.

"...and it was easy, really. I mean, I know the signs. So, when my brother started on how it was 'So Good Of Me To Come' and how he 'Hoped You've Finally Decided To Settle Down, I Can Find Work For You Here...' took me about three shifts to decide that I really couldn't do it..."

"...one of those jobs where you sit watching a monitor all day long and if you see an intruder you gotta call in the local police force. I mean why couldn't I go down and just shoot 'em or throw 'em out? But no that's not the way it works there..."

Miri leaned against the door of the truck, eyes on Skel. The Aus called him scrawny...but they called everyone scrawny, or worse. Skel was like the rest of the universe: taller than Miri by at least a half head. His arms were as free of fat as the rest of his body. He wasn't muscular in the body-sculpting sense but was close to having that kind of strength.

"Skel," she asked him when he took a breath. "why aren't you a captain? I mean, what are you *this* trip? Acting corporal?"

"C'mon, Miri. What would I want to be captain for? Just make me more of a target. No, not captain. Actually, on the chain of command I think they put me a little ahead of you, except all by myself. I'm Courier Class Five."

Miri laughed now.

"Last I looked you could only get to Class Four as Courier."

The truck found its way to the top of the hill, started wending its way down another steep incline.

"Really, Miri. I'm Courier Class Five. Means I have to try to do for transport what Joey does for weapons. Recognize, it figure it out, see if we should use it. That's why I'm driving this trip."

"But you oughta be in charge of something....".

"I am – in charge o'me. Take it light on me, huh? You sound like my brother. Well. Almost. "

She didn't say anything. He broke the sudden silence.

"Aw, Miri, I wasn't yelling at you. It's just that. . .I can't do it. I tried before you ever joined up. I was Sergeant. I was even a brevet Lieutenant once. . .but it won't stick. I'm just not cut that way."

"I hear you, soldier." she said. "I said the same thing about me, too."

"Yeah. Well. But see, you, you're young enough to learn. I'm not cut out to learn at my age. Falling apart, body and soul."

She didn't bother to stifle the the laugh.

"Not that body."

He looked hurt.

"You ain't seen this body in. . .months. Maybe years. It's getting old, kid."

"I hear you. I hear you. "

"No really. I can prove it!"

"Hell, it was *old* the first time I saw it..." Miri said.

"Now that's not true. I was only. . .when *was* that?"

"Skel, how long *could* it be? I've been with the Lunatics since. . .well, that was local years. Just about five Standards now. "

"So that means you're pushing about twenty-five Standards. Me? I'm older than that. I was twenty-five when I joined up more'n seventeen Standards back."

"Um. . .Skel? Who says I'm about twenty-five?"

Miri had to wait for his answer as he wrestled once more with the controls, producing a strange grinding noise from within the chassis.

"Stands to logic, kid. You sure can't be thirty yet, and maybe you're twenty-four."

"Yeah. Well guess you might think that. Now Heathrow is *old*, wouldn't you say? He's at least fifty, that's what I think. . ."

"Miri. You trying to hold something back on ol' Skel now? How old are you? If you don't mind me asking? You know I don't go round bragging on confidences. It really don't matter to me if you are thirty, or even thirty-five. You're Miri, that's all."

She choked back a half-laugh.

"Skel, I'm, oh damn. . .I'm about. . .well, a little shy yet, of twenty Standards, I'd say."

"That won't fadge Miri! That've meant you'd have been, say, fifteen Standards—less if you're shy on twenty now—the first time we ever messed around for a night."

"Yeah. I know. That's about right."

There was a silence. Miri took the opportunity to look out on the sudden view: mountains ahead, to the right and left a long green covered valley, and in the bottom of the valley a straight, deep-flowing river.

"Come on kid. I mean, you wouldn't have been legal. . .least not where I come from. I'm no Joey."

They both laughed.

"No, you're no Joey. That's sure. And I like you, Skel, always have. But I come from Surebleak. Yeah. Well. Born there, I was. Grew up there, too. Liz had a place there—you know that—she used it sometimes when she was waiting for multi-unit mixes to get together. She knew my mother. . .and Robertson too. Skel, didn't I ever tell you this stuff?"

"On the kynak, Miri. Not once. None of it."

"No. Guess not. Anyhow, that's it. Liz got me a chance to get off world. So I got."

"Ho. That's it? And then sweet, tiny Miri took the whole command by storm. And you were so quick. And you killed that idiot—what was his name?"

"Malter. Corporal Malter. " She supplied the name, barely recalled the incident, though. It hadn't been the first time someone had assumed such a small person was defenseless.

"And I got you drunk and you took me back with you because you were still shaking."

"I was going to leave you at the door, Skel. I really was. The idiot had been demanding part of my rations, and I'd thought I was out of all that. And he pushed me. Pulled a goddam stunner on me. I was still scared Skel, and it just seemed a good thing."

"No," she said suddenly, "it *was* a good thing, to have a friend. You're hardly old at all, Skel."

"My pleasure. Do it again, too. But damn, Miri, I mean you took it so good, really. It's one thing when you're fighting a war. But this guy. . .you did the right thing. You had to fight back. . .but you know that."

"Yeah. Seems like it keeps happening to me. You heard about Brum?"

The truck rumbled on a few moments.

"I took her in irons to the transshipment point. She and a bunch of cargo are waiting for a couple of weeks to C40 someplace else. She shouldn't pulled such a stupid thing. If I was there I'd have shot her in the back—combat soled shoes!"

"No, Skel. You wouldn't have. Happened pretty fast. Hmmm. Maybe you would have. You always see what's really happening."

"Maybe not. Not if you weren't fifteen Standards yet."

"Let it go, Skel. Not important. You were important. I came off of Surebleak. I'd already ki—already been in some tough spots. I didn't act like the kids on the high class planets. Besides, I didn't give you much of a choice, I think."

He laughed this time.

"Always can say no, Miri. Always have that choice when it comes to sharing joy. . .but I've always had a weakness for redheads."

"Always had a weakness for joy, you mean," she said.

"Camp coming up. Look smart: now you're the expert on the territory!"

"You ignoring me?" she asked as he shifted through the gears one last time.

"Naw, Miri. Just don't have a good answer to that one that's all."

"All out!" he yelled as the truck came to skidding halt. "All out!"

11

HER TROOPS WERE FINALLY situated. Miri walked slowly around the perimeter of their camp, trying to decide what was bothering her. It wasn't the ache: that was still with her and she knew it for what it was. No, it was something about the camp.

To begin with it seemed odd that Heathrow was in charge tonight and that she'd been scheduled to see Liz the following afternoon. Still, she didn't know everything. Maybe there were pressing things calling on Liz's time.

Something else tickled at the back of her mind.

The camp itself wasn't substantially changed from the day they'd dropped. The roads were plainer now from use, as were the paths around the camp: that was natural. The quarters were now defended by earthworks, but that would have happened anyway; it was nearly automatic to put walls up.

Ah. That was it. There weren't earthworks elsewhere: just around the quarters.

Anyone watching might assume that the Lunatics were digging in for a long stay, making things permanent. Instead it could be torn down in less than an hour. The earthworks were to give the soldiers something to do. Until they moved . Which might be anytime.

"Damn." Miri said softly and without conviction. For good measure she added several other expletives, none with force behind them.

Her "weather machine" was operating: she was rereading the manual for the third or fourth time, and still feeling as if she were missing some important instruction that would, by itself, cure the equipment of its inaccuracy.

The wind had turned colder: that's what had inspired her to check the equipment in the first place. Now the reading was for snow. The sky was slightly cloudy; what clouds there were seemed bent on a u-turn slightly to the west of the camp.

Bent to her task, Miri didn't notice the meaning of time every five minutes she took a new reading, compared it with the one before, compared the forecasts. . .

Now the sky was turning darker, and with it, her mood. The wind whipped in from the east solidly now. The clouds swept past at higher speeds, getting denser.

Now the forecast was for rain. Lots of rain.

The wind shifted again. With it came a few quick drops of rain and an occasional snowflake. Then just a blustery breeze: the drops stopped coming.

BOOM! Came the thunder from overhead.

As if aimed at the camp came the rain. One moment nothing, the next a heavy pouring, drenching torrent.

Miri leaned into the equipment. it at least, was waterproof. The sound was deafening and the flash of lightning repeatedly slashed at the pale late afternoon.

Then, a touch on her shoulder.

A dark form leaned into her in the rain she couldn't recognize at first.

". . .fool stunt is this, dammit, Miri? Come on with me!"

She made nodding motions, quickly shut the equipment down. She stood, felt a hand unexpectedly on her own.

"Skel?" Now she could see who it was.

He pulled on her hand and she followed, hand above her eyes to ward off the stinging rain.

The noise was a distant beat suddenly; she nearly fell into the relative silence of the room.

"What were you trying to do!" He was yelling." Look at you!"

She looked down and began laughing: "I got wet, Skel!"

"Wet behind the ears, dammit. I'm likely to believe that story of yours–here!"

He handed her a blanket and a towel.

"Get in there and get dry. Can't imagine what your troops will think about a sergeant not smart enough to get out of the rain! Ought to–dunno what I ought to."

He was pointing to the back section of his quarters.

"Look at you ! You're as wet as me!"

She took the towel in her hand, knocked his cap to the ground with it, and began dabbing at his hair.

"You get dry first." He started to argue, instead turned the effort to picking her up—and her reactions countered the move—and in a moment they were wrestling, and in the next, wet shirt against her face, Miri saw Skel's face clearly. Full of concern. Interest. Care.

"At ease, at ease." she whispered.

She was half on her back when she stopped resisting...and let his momentum carry him past her on the hard-packed floor.

She pounced then, throwing her tiny weight at him carefully.

"You're pinned Skel." she said seriously. " You wanna prove how old you are?"

"Redhead, you sure?"

She laughed, nibbled momentarily on his nose, and stood up.

"What do you think? " she asked as she started to slip out of her soggy blouse. "Gotta bed in here somewhere?"

The roar of the rain was a shield. For the first time in weeks Miri was more than an arm's length from a gun or knife; for the first time in weeks she was unconcerned about her troops. The weather equipment could stay where it was—nobody would bother it and she needn't be bothered with it either.

Miri, considering the noises they'd both made, was glad for the privacy. It was difficult being alone among the mercs, difficult to be both private and unrestrained. Paulia had yet to learn; assumed that somehow the closing of a metal door was enough distance.

This, this was almost luxury. Easily as private as the most expensive R&R resort she'd ever been to.

Of course Skel had been there, too. She'd invited him and footed the bills for the fling. Skel hadn't asked the cost: that would have been rude. As it was she'd spent all the bonus money and three quarters of the year's regular pay on those five days. In truth, worth every bit of it.

Here, today, was Skel. Skel who knew Miri's delight and joy with herself, Skel who appreciated her demands. For that matter, it was Skel who'd helped her discover some of her favorite things in those fervent days.

And it had been Skel who had carefully explained to her that love and lust within the Lunatics was not an easy thing; it required both patience and dignity to arrange liaisons in the field or it took neither.

For those who lacked patience and dignity there was always someone willing to take a few minutes or so for a bit of quick pleasure. That had always been too much like Surebleak for Miri, though, too much like the woman who'd lived downstairs from her for half-a-Standard and whose loud passionate moans could be heard every half-hour during the working day.

For those with dignity and patience there were good people; honestly giving and taking pleasure and joy and comfort without demanding more. That too, had been a hard lesson to learn. As close as one got, as many special private joys might be shared, there was always one or two or three someone elses . Unless full-partnered and willing to be part of that more-than-married state of bliss there *had* to be someone else. Being a mercenary was not an easy job, nor a safe one. More than a fifth of new recruits were hurt on the first mission, more than a half of those died. Skel moved against her, half asleep.

"Hello, Redhead. Thought you'd be gone."

"Not gone yet. Still got some itches need to be scratched. D'you know that hardly anyone I know really likes this?"

She reached around him with arms, began using her mouth on his neck. In a moment Skel was awake, and in a moment or two the figures looked like that sculpture she'd admired so much back at her first R&R resort.

The rain was a shield, the night a cloak, the joy an art.

Klamath was unaware.

Shan and Priscilla Ride Again

For the next few weeks—aka through August 3, with one week off (the week of June 8) because, Book Tour, we will be posting a chapter from *Shan and Priscilla Ride Again* on Splinter Universe. The reason it's 16 weeks for 15 chapters is because there is a prologue.

Shan and Priscilla Ride Again is a Liaden novel which was never finished, though it was written out to 15 chapters (about 22,000 words).

For more information, and to start in on the fun, here's the Authors' Introduction to the Outtake Chapters.

Introduction to Shan and Priscilla Ride Again

I believe we may have mentioned in the past that, originally, Steve and I had intended to do a direct sequel to *Conflict of Honors*, following Shan and Priscilla on their own timeline, until it intersected with Val Con and Miri in the book we know now as *Carpe Diem*.

Unfortunately, that sequel was never completed; Priscilla and Shan's story became secondary to Miri and Val Con's over-the-top adventures, and so the universe has taken on the shape it now has.

I say, note, that the sequel to *Conflict* was never completed. We did, however, begin to write it, and I, at least, had mostly forgotten about it, until I got into the file cabinets in order to move Stuff into boxes to go to the archives at NIU.

But, here it is, working title *Shan and Priscilla Ride Again*, with a start date at the top of Chapter One, written in what used to be my hand, in that green ink I used to favor: *start approx 9/26/86*

September 26, 1986. My charmingly low-tech card file tells me that we submitted *Conflict of Honors* to Del Rey on September 17, 1986. Looks like we took a week off to recover, and got right back down to it.

Ah, youth. Such *energy*.

The card file also tells me that we sent a proposal and the first 60 pages of the book that would become *Carpe Diem* to Del

Rey on November 3, 1987. Our editor expressed Extreme Doubt, and strongly suggested that we write something else. Something. . .serious. Let go of this space opera nonsense before people thought that we weren't capable of writing anything. . .good.

The next notation on the *Carpe Diem* page indicates that we sent the completed manuscript to Del Rey on October 3, 1988.

Now, along with the manuscript with the 1986 date at the top of Chapter One, there are handwritten notes, with another date—August 8, 1988. So, it looks like *Carpe Diem* went to Steve for his go-through, and I opened up *Shan and Priscilla Ride Again*, immediately, and began to try to recapture the magic.

I should mention that a lot happened between October 3, 1988, and November 17, 1988, the date on which we received a grumpy acceptance letter from the editor at Del Rey, indicating that our agent had had to exert all of her powers of persuasion to achieve that acceptance.

In fact, we had sold much of what we owned, and moved to Maine, arriving just in time for the first snowfall of October.

Moving house is an adventure. Shifting our base of operations from the state we had both lived in for all of our lives to that point (Steve was 38; I was 36) to a Whole 'Nother State was. . .almost overwhelming. We had to regroup on almost every level, and when we had finally found a place to live (to replace the house we had rented long-distance, and which arrangement had fallen through as we were on the road north), and day-jobs, it was December, and the revision letter for *Carpe Diem* reached us from Del Rey, asking us, among other things, to cut out the beginning of Pat Rin's run and the segue into what is now *I Dare*. We returned the revised manuscript in January 1989, and the book was eventually published in October 1989.

And in all that rush, and the subsequent writing of *The Tomorrow Log*, to satisfy Del Rey's option clause, and our editor's adamance that we write something that *was not* Liaden—*Shan and Priscilla Ride Again* got lost.

What we have is about 22,000 words of novel, and two outtake chapters. We'll be posting the chapters one every week until they run out, for your interest, and, frankly, for ours.

The chapters following *are* interesting, for a number of reasons, not the least of which is that we get to see Val Con before he became an Agent of Change.

Have fun!

Prologue

Healer Hall
Solcintra, Liad
Year Named Glafiim

E r Thom yos'Galan sat rigid in the comfortable chair, resisting the caress of the cushions; hands fisted on the soft arm rests. It was scarcely a posture one would expect of the second-most important person on the planet, though Er Thom rarely thought of himself in those terms. True enough, he was Korval-in-Trust. Equally true, he was Thodelm yos'Galan, as well as Captain and Master Trader of *Dutiful Passage*.

An awesome *melant'i*, in whole or in parts. Certainly a man who juggled such burdens could ease back into the chair and await the Master Healer with calm.

Except that this was Shan—his eldest; his heir; dearly loved, if little understood. Er Thom filled his lungs and forced stiff muscles to relax into the cushions. Whatever had happened—whatever was amiss—he would not add shame to his son's miseries.

The door across from him slid open and Er Thom was on his feet, bowing with haste to the sudden small woman; who smiled and inclined her head respectfully.

"Lord yos'Galan."

"Master Healer."

He heard the note of dread in his voice; recalled that the Healer had direct access to the din of his emotions, and was oddly comforted.

She came forward slowly, and stood looking up at him for a heartbeat or two, dark eyes thoughtful; hands folded loosely before her.

"Your son is a Healer," she said at last, in the neutral tones of one instructing.

A Healer. Well, and such things were not unknown within the clan. Er Thom awaited further instruction.

The Master Healer smiled.

"We have tested him and find he is not only capable of hearing the emotions of others, but also of the control necessary to be an active Healer. It would be best for him to stay here until he is trained in shielding and in such techniques as he can master. This has been explained to him."

She paused, glanced up into the man's violet eyes; read the matrix of his concern and added.

"He resists the notion of staying with us. Strongly."

Humor glimmered through him, barely touching lips and eyes. "I see."

He paused and the Master Healer caught the hum of concentrated thought.

"How long must he remain? The course of study—"

"Varies with every individual. Your son is—quick; and stronger than is usually found among those just come halfling. . ."

"Halfling." He looked stricken, then shook his head, Terran-wise. "Yes, of course."

She waited, weighing the wisdom of untangling his knots of confusion and offering him comfort. As she watched, one knot fell apart of itself, the purple buzz of concentration very audible.

The Master Healer composed herself to wait. The boy must have the training—for his own sake and the sake of those he encountered throughout his adult life. Quick—she nearly laughed. During the initial probe, she had reached far within him, as one must, past the current upset to the deeper self, searching out imbalances, inadequacies. She had brushed rather too closely to that heart place and had suddenly found herself the target of a bolt of concentrated outrage that one scarcely expected from an untrained adult, must less a frightened boy. Her shield was barely up in time.

Later, she had attempted to subdue a particularly violent bit of temper with a bolt of her own—only to see him fling a clumsy, but recognizable, shield into place.

Gods protect an old woman from such quickness.

Er Thom yos'Galan stirred.

"He must learn to control this ability. I see that. I would be—more comfortable for the clan—were he tutored at home."

"Forgive me," she murmured, pitying him. "Teaching must be done away from the noise of those unshielded." She smiled slightly. "There is progression, Your Lordship. We do not wish to overburden him. We wish to help him gain control of his new eyes and use them to see as far as he might."

"Of course." He seemed about to say more; but in the end did not. The Master Healer hesitated.

"As I mentioned, sir, your son does not take the suggestion that he remain with us for training seriously. He demands to be allowed to go home. I thought, perhaps, if you spoke to him; explained necessity. . ."

Another glint of humor, wholly unexpected.

"Ah. I will be pleased to speak with my son, Master Healer."

She bowed thanks and he moved past her, pilot smooth, heading for the door.

SHAN SPUN TOWARD HIM, light eyes huge in a ravaged brown face.

"Father?" Then, with furious passion. "Father, I don't want to be a Healer! I want to go on *Dutiful Passage* and be a trader! You said I could—you *promised*! The year I turn twelve, you said. This trip! And now it's time to go and that—person!—says I must stay here and be a Healer, only because I cried when Obre cut herself and was frightened—and I *told* her I wouldn't do it again! I *won't* do it again, Father, I—"

"Shan."

It broke the flow, but not the passion. The boy flung forward, big hands outstretched.

"Father, please!"

Er Thom took the thin face between gentle hands, looked into silver eyes level with his own. *Only twelve, gods. . .* He would be Terran-high, after all. Like his mother. Er Thom stroked his thumbs gently down the prisoned cheeks.

"Shan. Peace for a moment, my child. Listen to the why. It is true that I gave my word. But I could not know you would come halfling, nor what that would bring you. To be a Healer does not mean you cannot become a trader. It merely means that you cannot begin your training this trip. Mastering the Healer's skills must come first for you."

"No. No—Father, I'll come here after the *Passage* comes back. I'll learn *then*."

"I will not have my ship endangered!"

Shan froze between his hands. Suddenly, shockingly, he began to cry.

He never cries. . .

But he had cried, yesterday, with Obre's pain—and now,today. Did he cry with his father's distress, Er Thom wondered, or his own? He gathered the thin body close, rubbing his golden cheek against the wet brown one.

"Hush, *denubia*. Hush, my child; my heart. . ."

The boy cried harder; hard, breaking sobs, as if he fought each one. Er Thom cuddled him tight.

"Listen, *denubia*. Hear how it might be. You, walking in a strange port. Suddenly an accident occurs nearby—someone is badly injured by a piece of machinery. You cry out as you did with Obre. If the port is new to the *Passage*, there could be no trouble, or mild trouble, or very great trouble. The galaxy is wide; and custom is strange. In such a case, you endanger not only yourself, but the ship and the person who is injured."

It seemed to him that the boy in his arms was somewhat quieter.

"Stay and learn what the Master Healer has to each and you may at least save yourself the grief of another's pain. At most, you might aid those in need." He paused, doubtful. "Do you understand why this lesson must come first?"

Silence, then a cracked mumble; a clearing of the throat and a muffled, "Yes, Father."

"Good. Then you know that the Captain does not deny you your heritage. He merely postpones it."

Shan snuffled and pulled away, rubbing a sleeve across stark cheeks. Er Thom silently offered a handkerchief.

"How long will I have to—stay here?"

"Until you have learned what you must know to be safe." Er Thom hesitated, considering.

"If you learn quickly, and well, I will leave instructions at home that you may begin piloting lessons when you return."

"Father!" Er Thom found himself hugged with undignified violence.

"Only if you attend what you are taught here, and learn with good nature."

"I will—I will, Father. Oh, thank you!"

Er Thom lifted a hand to stroke his son's bright white hair, and smiled, sadly.

"Do not thank me, child. It is what you must learn, too."

Auctorial Reflections

ONE OF THE MOST STRIKING things about this piece, to me, is that, in the later stories, Er Thom's children often comment on how much of a trial he had been to them: cool, exacting, and stern. It was to their mother, Anne Davis, Er Thom's Terran lifemate, that the children looked for tenderness and understanding.

Yet, in the above narrative, we see Er Thom as being frightened for his child, and tender in the face of Shan's fear and temper. We do see something of Er Thom's own temper, when he's struck on one of Korval's nerves—*I will not have my ship endangered!*—but he recovers himself quickly and returns to comforting and reasoning with the child.

I believe that this is our first glimpse of Er Thom "in person" as it were, produced well before *Local Custom* and *Scout's Progress*, which were written in 1992 and 1993, respectively.

I will also comment, just briefly, that the words you are reading in this, and coming, chapters are the exact words that are on the old pages; we're not editing as we go along—except for One Single Thing.

Apparently, in 1986/1988, neither one of us had quite grasped the rules of paragraphing with regard to dialog and following action. I have inserted paragraph breaks, in order to make the text more readable, on-screen.

Sharon Lee
April 13, 2015

Chapter One

He really was quite beautiful.

Priscilla paused, aware that she was staring. Quite beautiful. Slim and golden-skinned, green eyes bright under straight brows partially hidden by a fall of glossy dark hair. He held himself with careless grace and moved with an economy of motion that spoke volumes of efficiency. He was a shade taller than Pat Rin yos'Phelium, with whom he was speaking, and, unlike that gentleman, wore the very minimum of jewelry required by so exalted a gathering. The effect was not one of inelegance, however. Something in the younger man's bearing made the exquisite and bejeweled Pat Rin seem just a trifle—overdone.

At that moment, the object of her study turned and caught her eyes upon him. One straight brow slid upward, to be hidden completely by the renegade lock of hair.

Priscilla felt herself flush.

"I do beg your pardon," she said, half-laughing. "It's just that I was thinking how much you look like Captain yos'Galan."

"Look like Shan?" Pat Rin's voice carried a subtle note of shock.

His companion raised his glass, second brow rising to join the first. "No, don't you think so?"

"No one looks like Shan!" Pat Rin announced with accuracy, but without, perhaps, tact. Priscilla felt the electric tingle of the young gentleman's irritation as if it were her own.

Lacking her advantages, Pat Rin pushed on. "You look more like me than you look like Shan!"

Which was strictly correct. But the similarity she had seen was more than a superficial likeness of hair color or even facial structure. It had to do with bearing, with efficiency of motion. With assuredness. She was pondering how best to explain this when Pat Rin suddenly recalled himself.

"Do forgive me, Lady. Here is my cousin, Val Con yos'Phelium. Kinsman, here is Priscilla Delacroix y Mendoza."

She smiled and bowed acknowledgment blended with equality, for warmth. "Lord yos'Phelium. You're a Scout?"

He returned her bow exactly, lips twitching.

"Lady Mendoza. Indeed I am. Have you been acquainted with my brother long?"

"Only a few relumma," she said carefully.

"Lady Mendoza serves as first mate on *Dutiful Passage*," Pat Rin informed his cousin.

"Ah. Then I am very pleased to meet you, indeed, Lady. My sister was to bring me to call on you. In Balance I was constrained to escort her this evening, since she cried out that she was too timid to go alone."

This did not sound a great deal like either of his foster-sisters, in Priscilla's opinion.

Nor in Pat Rin's.

"Anthora?" he asked, clearly puzzled. "She's nearly always by herself. Not for lack of offered escorts, either. I'm forever meeting her."

The green eyes were very bright.

"Are you? Well, perhaps because it's my first day at home in a relumma or two. No doubt she felt I would expire of boredom if I were—"

"There you are!" Anthora yos'Galan slid her arm through her foster-brother's. "Well met, kinsman. Priscilla—how are you, my friend? Will you dislike it excessively if I bring Val Con with me tomorrow evening?"

"Of course not. I'll be happy to have him."

"That's very good, then." Anthora tugged on Val Con's arm. "There's someone I want you to meet, Brother."

"I thought as much," he murmured, soft voice resigned. "Nova employees an agent these days, does she?"

"What can you be talking about?" Anthora wondered, light eyes innocent.

Her brother sighed. "I am speaking at this present with Lady Mendoza."

"Yes, but you see, Priscilla must go to Lady Faaldom now, and I'm certain Pat Rin would rather court Tabita sig'Renlin; so you're bereft in anywise."

Priscilla grinned, catching a bright green eye.

"It seems we each have our orders, sir."

"So it does." He frowned at Anthora, a feat of pure willpower, since within he was bubbling bright, exasperated mirth.

"I hear you come most frequently alone to parties. Pat Rin says he's always meeting you."

"Oh, now, not *always*," she protested. "It can't be *always*, you know, kinsman."

"Now, cousin, admit that I see you everywhere," Pat Rin chided.

"But I can't, cousin."

She turned back to her brother.

"I go so many places that he doesn't, you see," she explained earnestly.

Val Con exploded into laughter.

Grinning, Anthora bore him off.

Auctorial Reflections

I HAD A REALLY, *really* hard time not editing the heck out of this chapter. It needs—oh, so very much. Polish, grace, *detail*.

I'm particularly displeased with the portrayal of Pat Rin, who would *never* have been so gauche, nor so publicly disdainful of another Korval clan member, no matter how much he was secretly horrified.

On the other hand, this little scene represents our first attempt to fumble toward the notion of the "clan face." Which is to say that the various members of a clan will tend to resemble each other, even if they don't particularly *look like* each other, because of the similarity of upbringing, and the clan's internal culture.

Sharon Lee

April 20, 2015

Chapter the Second

Vaslin House
Pelthraza Street, Solcintra

The house was crowded. Her house.

Her *home*.

Priscilla smiled, hugging the thought to herself. How strange, after so many years of having had none at all, to suddenly possess two homes, equally dear, equally new, equally wondrous.

Riches beyond all counting. *Thanks be, Mother.*

Thanks be, too, for those that filled the tiny gather-room, spilling out into the cramped city-house garden.

Her friends.

Goddess, I'm a wealthy woman.

A stir at the entranceway: Teyas ushering in a group of late-coming guests.

Priscilla started forward to perform the host's duty—and her grin broadened

Four distinctive individuals were following the butler into the hall: the women as unalike each other as the men. Yet one could not deny they were a family.

Anthora, dark-haired, plump, and silver-eyed, come in on the arm of her eldest sister, Nova, a slyphlike symphony of golden hair and serious amethyst eyes. Behind them, young Val Con, tipping his head back to address some comment to the tall, white-haired man at his side. Priscilla's smile softened at the sight of the stark, wing-browed face and she lengthened her stride.

"Friends."

"Priscilla!" Anthora was laughing. "What a lot of people! We left our gifts in the hallway with the others, since you weren't there—"

"For which she is not to be chided," Nova frowned. "We are at fault, for arriving late."

"*Shan's* at fault," Anthora corrected spiritedly.

"I beg your pardon? I'll inform you, young lady, that I cut business short today in order to be home in good time—"

"And then spent *hours* dressing!" she retored hotly. "Truly, Shan-brother, one would have thought you bound for contract-troth!"

Shan considered her from under astonished brows before turning to the silent man at his side.

"As much as it must naturally grieve me to say such a thing, brother, it occurs to me that sister is a blatherskite."

"No, do you say so?" Val Con turned a bright green gaze upon Anthora. "What's to be done, I wonder?"

"We might," suggested Shan very seriously, "drown her."

"It seems extreme," the younger man commented thoughtfully. "How if we simply refuse to allow her in company?"

"She might then wither away to dust," Nova chimed in unexpectedly. "Kinder to drown, I think, brothers."

"We do," Shan allowed, "owe kindness to our kin."

Priscilla felt anger rising in Anthora as the younger woman grew more embarrassed. Carefully, lest the other take it amiss, she extended a tendril along the inner pathways: warm welcome heavily laced with calm. Anthora relaxed visibly. Made a small, not completely ungrudging bow.

"Forgive me, Shan-brother. It was not my intent to discomfort you."

"Well, that's certainly a relief!" he said, but at the same time proffered his own touch of affection, leaching any sting from the words. "Why don't you hoodlums make your bows to the host and then leave us in peace for a moment?"

They did so as if they were biddable children, which they emphatically, Priscilla thought, were not. Val Con augmented his very pretty salutation with an upcast flash of smile that was absurdly unsettling.

"Shall I give you an introduction to my brother, Priscilla?" Shan teased her in soft Terran.

"Thank you," she replied composedly. "Pat Rin has already done so."

"Cheated of what little service I might render!" He cried in mock anguish, so that Lady yo'Lanna's head turned toward them. His emotive pattern, familiar and dear, sparkled mischief, and affection, and desire—

And Priscilla laughed—at him, at herself, at the two of them. Slipping an arm through his, she steered him toward the refreshment table.

"You look perfectly miserable without a glass in your hand. Let's at least take care of that. Then we can find a more or less quiet place and you can tell me what I can do for you."

"As obvious as that? A glass of the red would be delightful—it *is* the red Nova sent from our cellar, isn't it?"

"It is. At first, I couldn't understand why she would provide wine for a party where she was an invited guest. But then I realized that it must be that you were only making sure that there would be something drinkable here, rather than trust my judgment of wine."

"I'd trust your judgment in anything, Priscilla," he said softly. "There's no need to beggar yourself for the affair, necessary as it is. yos'Galan's cellar is full." He poured himself a glass and raised it, saluting her with a smile. "Much better. Do you like being part of Liaden society?"

"Everyone's been very kind."

"What an extraordinary thing to say! Especially of Liadens. Out here, perhaps?" He led the way to the window and Priscilla followed him 'round the small patio to a corner thick with jazmin blossoms and shadow. The sounds of the party were suddenly distant. She sat on the low stone ledge and looked up at him.

"How may I serve you, Thodelm?"

He grimaced.

"By listening as my good friend—and as my first mate."

Having said that, he fell silent, sipping wine and staring at the pale jazmin flowers. Abruptly, he came and sat next to her.

"I had a pinbeam from my Uncle Richard—Gordy's grandfather." He paused.

Priscilla nodded. Gordon Arbuthnot had been cabin boy on the last voyage of the *Dutiful Passage*, Priscilla's first trip.

"It seems," Shan was saying, "that we did him more harm than good. The situation with the stepfather has not improved. In fact, it's my uncle's opinion that Gordy is less patient of the man than ever before."

"That happens," Priscilla commented. "It's part of growing up. Gordy was a member of the crew on the *Passage*, not a—not a *little boy...*"

"Precisely," Shan murmured, and was quiet again for a heartbeat or two.

"Katy-Rose—Gordy's mother—is caught between the two," he said eventually. "Worn to a frazzle, according to Uncle Richard, and ready to walk away from both. Morgan—again, according to Uncle Dick—is a good man, but a trifle narrow. Gordy's seen the Wide Universe." He sighed.

"In short, Uncle Richard would like us to have Gordy back."

Priscilla considered it.

"He's a good boy. Intelligent. Showed some talent for the trading, too, I thought."

Shan nodded.

"I think it's possible. But I do need the first mate's opinion on the subject." He hesitated. "It's as if the *Passage* is a clan, Priscilla, with the captain as delm and the first mate as delmae. Uncle Richard is asking us to take a fosterling into the clan, likely for more than this one trip. Gordy is ripe for halfling. . ."

She thought about that. Gordy was what? Twelve Standards? A changing time, in any case. And if his heart's desire was set aside now, with all the other changes. . .

"I see no reason," she said serenely, "why Gordy Arbuthnot should not be fostered as a son into our clan."

A jolt of—something—from him, and the look he turned on her was more passion than delight.

"Oh, Priscilla. . ."

Her grip on the crystal cup was dangerous. She loosened it and drew a shaky breath.

"Are the reasons still good?"

"Good. . ." He sighed. "Merely difficult."

A sudden laugh.

"Gods, how wise I've become!"

He touched her hand.

"About this other thing, Priscilla. Will you come with me to Uncle Richard? It might set Katy-Rose's mind at rest if she sees what a fine, upstanding and calm person I have as my first mate."

"Certainly, I'll come," she told him, beginning the sequence to slow her racing heart. "When do we leave?"

Auctorial Reflections

IT WOULD HAVE BEEN really cool, having made *such* a point about how much time Shan took with his toilette, to *actually see what he was wearing.* Oh, well, maybe we would have thought of that during the second draft.

It would have also been nice if we had unzipped this a little further, to recap the point at issue between Priscilla and Shan. Which is that they have agreed to run the *Passage* together for an entire trade trip before they allow themselves to become lovers. At least we managed to remember to tell people who Gordy Arbuthnot is.

Also? We see Shan pour a glass of wine for himself, but he doesn't seem to have poured one for Priscilla, which is unexpectedly boorish of him, but apparently doesn't actually matter, because she's miraculously come up with a glass on her own sometime during their discussion in the garden.

"Wing-browed" has *got* to go.

Val Con does seem to be flirting rather pointedly with his brother's girlfriend. I'd wonder what's with that, exactly, except that we've already read the outtake chapters. *Now* I wonder if we forgot to remove the build-up to a scene that no longer exists, or if we Had a Better Idea.

Sharon Lee
April 26, 2015

Chapter the Third

Celbridge-on-the-Louch
New Dublin

"No."

The boy's tone was calm, and utterly certain. Morgan chose to understand that it was also insolent.

"And it's 'yes' I've told you this minute gone by, my boy, and 'yes' I'll be having from you. Did you learn nothing on that fancy star-goer of yours about obedience to the elder?"

The reference to *Dutiful Passage* was unfortunate. Katy-Rose looked up from the score she was studying, face tense. Gordy's shoulders tightened still more, but his only comment was a flat correction.

"Grandad's the elder. Not you."

Morgan clamped his jaw on the surge of temper.

"Nonetheless, I'm elder of you, besides being your ma's own husband, and your father-in-law. This is the last time I'm telling you. Get into working clothes. You're for your Uncle Edward this day. Time you did some honest labor!" He paused.

The lad stood motionless, except that his hands curled into fists at the end of his stiff arms. Morgan was reminded that Finn Arbuthnot had been a powerful man, in spite that he'd made his way by the music and the storytelling. He cleared his throat.

"Are you hearing me, Gordy? Or must I be taking you by force?"

"Morgan—" began his wife.

"You can't," Gordy stated clearly, voice rising so that it carried to the ceiling-corners. "Father-in-law you might be, and husband to my mother, but you're no father to my heart and I'll have none of you!"

"Gordon!" Katy-Rose was on her feet, bur Morgan was nearer.

"Can't, is it? I'll remind you, my lad, that you live as a dependent in this household and the law demands obedience from you on that count alone. Whether or not your heart is engaged!"

He grabbed Gordy's arm.

"It's to your uncle you're going today, if I have to carry you every step of the way!"

He yanked.

And gasped with shock. It was if the child were rooted to the floor.

Morgan readjusted his grip and pulled again. Harder.

Gordy remained rooted, brown eyes squinted in concentration, fair hair slightly damp across his forehead.

"Stop it!" Katy-Rose demanded, trying to push between husband and son. "Both of you, give over!"

But Morgan was angry—and who could blame him, with the boy so intractable? And who could blame *him*, with his stepfather after him all the day long, insisting that Gordy be doing something 'profitable' instead of—instead of. . .

Whatever it was that Gordy did.

The man had shifted his grip again, preparing to lift the boy. Katy-Rose saw in a moment of clarity that Gordy had gained inches; that he was less pudgy; that his face began now to show the shadows of the lines it would wear as a man.

"Morgan, let be!" Her voice was low, urgent.

She lay a hand on his shoulder. He shrugged it off, attention all for the boy.

The doorbell rang.

"Praise be!" she breathed and hurried to let rescue within.

Her father was there, smiling—rescue enough. But Katy-Rose stood staring in consternation at the two he brought with him, until—

"Shan! Priscilla!"

Gordy twisted easily from Morgan's frozen grip and ran forward, face full of joy.

The man bent gracefully, returning a brutal boy's hug fully, and laying his cheek against the soft hair.

"Gordy. It's good to see you, *achusla*."

But Gordy was already flinging away, wrapping his arms around the woman with no less abandon.

"Priscilla, Priscilla. . ."

"Hello, Gordy." The woman's voice was unexpectedly deep. A storyteller's voice, Katy-Rose understood, and spared a moment to wonder where this woman had trained to be a bard.

She was distracted in the next instant by the elegant sweep of the man's bow.

"Cousin. Housefather. I hope I see you in good health and in good heart."

"Health follows a joyous heart."

She gave the traditional response; managed a smile. "You command of our tongue improves."

"It's a demanding teacher your son is," murmured Shan, expanding his range a bit to scan nuance.

The man was obviously upset, even as he came forward to stand beside his wife; and Katy-Rose gave off alternating waves of sorrow, worry, relief, nervousness. A joyous heart, indeed. To the side, he heard Gordy, his pattern a mess of suppressed fury, longing, and genuine joy, speaking to Priscilla in Trade.

"I know I shouldn't have used the Tree against him, Priscilla. But I didn't *hit* him. . ."

She murmured something for his ears alone, and Shan detected the opening of a road of comfort between them, even as she began a Sort of the scrambled emotions. That was in hand, then.

"Well! Let's not all stand in the doorway like dummies, my dears!"

Uncle Richard's voice was loud enough to make Kay-Rose jump.

"Morgan, you'll be remembering my sister's own boy, Shan. And he's brought his first mate with him, the very Priscilla we've heard so much about, eh, Grandson?" He gestured, and switched to Terran, apparently assuming that Priscilla didn't have the local language.

"Ms. Mendoza, this will be my daughter, Katy-Rose Davis, and her husband, Morgan O'Clery. Come in, come in! Let's all sit and be comfortable."

Which was, Shan thought, a statement of optimism is ever he'd heard one. He stepped aside to let Uncle Dick show the way, noting how Morgan started and gave ground, as if the old man's intent had not been clearly announced. But, no—he recalled that the husband had very little Terran; and little use for it, to be just. A local man, working locally, what need had he to learn Terran?

No wonder Gordy lost patience.

SEATS HAD BEEN FOUND, pleasantries exchanged. Refreshments had been brought by a Gordy so eager to please that Morgan stared at him in disbelief. After serving the bowls all around, he came uninvited into the adults' circle, sitting on the rug between the two outworlders, eyes half-closed, as if basking in the sun.

Morgan frowned, and would have spoken, but Richard Davis raised a hand.

"The talk concerns the boy, as well. Let him stay."

Morgan subsided, though with ill grace. Gordy, cross-legged on the floor, was suddenly wide-eyed, scarcely seeming to breathe.

"Gordon."

"Yes, Grandad?"

The hope-filled eyes pinned Richard to his chair. Tension made a nails-on-slate squeal against a Healer's senses, and Shan narrowed his field of perception.

"It's that your cousin says he's willing to take you on again, should you be willing to go. Before we begin in detail, that is what I need to know. Are you willing?"

"Crelm! Yes—" He was half up, twisting around to speak to the man behind him. "Shan—please! I'll be—I'll study. I will! You won't have to—"

"Peace."

One big hand descended, resting lightly on the fair hair.

"I gather you're here on sufferance, Gordy; and I didn't ask you, your grandfather asked you. Strive for some conduct."

The mildest possible tone; one could hardly call it a rebuke at all, Katy-Rose thought. Yet Gordy swallowed and took a breath and turned with a bit of calmness to speak to his grandfather.

"Yes, sir. I'm willing—willing to go with Shan—" His voice broke and he stopped, all eyes and straining tension. Katy-Rose felt tears rising; looking to find her cousin's silver eyes on her, lean face full of sympathy.

"It's not unusual to foster a child into another Line—even into another clan. There's no reason not to offer aid."

He grinned.

"Besides, I may be asking for a return of the favor soon enough, Cousin. My daughter Padi bids fair to be a hell-raiser."

"I didn't know," she stammered, mindful that Morgan could not follow such a spate of Terran; "that it was as bad as that for him. . ."

"People grow. And sometimes they have needs and talents that are different from others in the family."

He extended a hand, the big purple ring glinting in the dim room-lights.

"It doesn't mean that love's gone away."

As if his words had the power of comfort, she took a breath. Another. And felt the tears recede. Hesitantly, she touched his fingertips, smiling a little as she turned away.

She caught Priscilla Mendoza's ebony eyes on her and wondered anew at the beauty of the woman: stormcloud curls and white, white skin; she might have set herself as a deliberate foil for her Captain, with his warm brown skin and seafroth hair. She nodded slightly, and the outworlder smiled like the sun rising. Katy-Rose gasped and instinctively sought Morgan's face.

But he was glowering, cut off by lack of language. He ignored her smile, and her hand, eyes fixed on Richard.

"That's settled, then, is it, Johnny Galen?"

"Yes, Uncle Dick," Shan said calmly. "That's settled."

"We'll put off the rest of this discussion until the morrow, if you've no objections to it. It's getting on to local evening, and an old man doesn't do his best trading late in the day."

The younger man threw his head back, and his laughter overflowed the circle.

"Have me believe you beyond your prime, will you? That's one's older than you are by several magnitudes, sir! But, let us by all means speak in the morning, if you feel it gives you an advantage."

Auctorial Reflections

AND HERE WE ARE AT New Dublin.

This chapter feels more solid to me than either of the first two chapters, which were kinda squishy around the edges. Finally, there's a story going on!

I do wish Gordy would cut poor Morgan some slack—not everyone can be expected to have received Gordy's advantages, after all. On the other hand, Gordy's in One of Those Difficult Times of Life, and, to be fair, Morgan is apparently no Finn Arbuthnot, who had been a bard, and, one gathers, Somewhat Larger Than Life. One wonders what Katy-Rose was thinking, to go from Larger Than Life to Steadfast and Earnest. Though Larger Than Life *is* occasionally wearing. Perhaps she was just looking for. . .less drama in her life.

Ahem.

Still haven't quite gotten control of the point-of-view/ head-hopping thing, but still—a good scene, pretty much everything that needs to be unzipped is, and we get a good tight look of what, exactly, is going on in Katy-Rose's household.

Given that we very often write material—up to a hundred pages, and no, we've never gotten entirely out of the habit—ahead of a book's proper beginning, this chapter may well *be* the "natural" chapter one.

Oh, and I do *like* Richard Davis.

Sharon Lee
May 3, 2015

Chapter the Fourth

Celbridge-on-the-Louch
New Dublin

"Uncle Richard."

The older man looked up from his breakfast grumpily, having not yet had his second cup of coffee.

"Johnny Galen."

"Do you know a firm named Porta Culthert?"

If Shan noticed the surliness, he gave no sign. And, truth told, thought Katy-Rose, it was rare you saw a man looking so rested, sitting there in all his finery, eating hotcakes and sausage as if it were all what he was accustomed to having. As she well knew it was not.

"Porta Culthert?" Richard frowned. "Michael Sullivan's little venture, isn't it? Sound enough people."

"Really? Well, that's a relief, don't you think, Priscilla? It would hardly do to be dealing with out and out thieves. But since a sound enough fellow asks me to call—"

Gordy looked up from his plate. "Asked you to call?"

Katy-Rose frowned at him, but his eyes were on the outworlders, not on her.

"To be sure," Shan agreed, eyebrows lifting. "Does that meet with your approval, Gordon? Should I clear all my interviews with you beforehand?"

Gordy did not dignify this with an answer. Instead, he asked, "What does he want to see you about?"

"About? He did want to see me about something. I recall that distinctly. Perhaps he wants to marry Nova? No, that wasn't it. . .That's not the fellow who's so eager to buy the *Passage*, is it, Priscilla? I do wish you would attend to some of these details. . ."

"Michael Sullivan wanted to speak with you about whiskey, Captain." The woman's voice was smooth and untroubled. "I believe he meant to offer you a deal."

"That was it! Prime whiskey, made according to the old Irish recipe, in oak barrels, to be shipped entire. Not a bad notion. And his opening price was nearly reasonable, wasn't it, Priscilla?"

"You said," murmured the woman, leveling ebony eyes at him over the rim of her coffee cup, "that you'd net enough profit to set up a chain of pleasure-houses in the Eighth Quadrant."

"Did I say that? Must have been in my cups."

"Very likely."

"No, wait—"

Gordy touched the man's hand where it lay on the linen cloth.

"Shan—you don't want to buy whiskey from Mike Sullivan."

"I don't? Your grandfather assures me he's a very sound fellow."

"Yeah, but. . . If he's setting the deal at more than a hundred bits the keg, he's playing you for a know-nothing."

The light eyes were speculative.

"Explain."

Gordy squirmed.

"Well, see, he's been buying up all the stock whiskey for a couple months, local. Since I got back, maybe. And then he started buying margins. I'd bought futures from Dunlevie for fifty bits the keg. Next thing I knew, Mike Sullivan was leaving me word that he'd buy what I had for seventy."

"Gordy. . ." This has gone far enough. Morgan would not be pleased if he came home from the morning's work to find the boy so deep in conversation with adults.

"No. Cousin, I ask your indulgence. The information is of some value to me."

She stared at him in surprise. The buffoonery was gone from voice and face. She glanced out the window, but Morgan was not yet in sight.

"All right, then."

"Thank you, Cousin." He moved his attention. "Well, Gordy? Did you sell?"

"For seventy? Crelm!" Gordy snorted. "I told him eighty-five and took eighty. But, Shan—he bought everything! I had a little reserve and three cantra's worth of futures—"

"You had what?" Katy-Rose could barely believe her ears. "Buying three cantra's worth of whiskey? As if whiskey hadn't brought enough grief to your life, now you'll be beggaring your family!"

"Peace, Daughter. The boy won his gamble. Let him finish."

Richard looked completely awake, all attention on Gordy.

"Father—"

"Ma, I *made* money! I didn't beggar us at all!"

"But you could have." Shan's voice was very serious. "Three cantra on futures, Gordy? That's rather a big bite, isn't it?"

"Shan, I was sure!"

The white-haired man grinned suddenly.

"Remind me to tell you a few stories about times when I was sure." The grin faded. "How did you manage it? No glossing, please; you know that Priscilla loves details."

Gordy glanced uncertainly at the first mate. She smiled at him.

"It does seem like a great deal of money, Gordy. Where did you get it?"

"It's mine! My pay from the *Passage* and the cuts I got from the spec cargo and the finder's fees. I made *six* cantra last trip. An' Grandad said I could have three, and three had to be put in trust for me."

"So you decided to gamble your entire investment account on whiskey futures. . ." Shan said, prompting gently.

Gordy shrugged impatiently.

"I paid them a third. If something went wrong, I had the rest in the account. And I figured the dividends from the stocks would pay the fees." He leaned forward. "I was sure! And it worked! I came out with *five* cantra, instead of three!"

"Or none," Priscilla said. She sipped her coffee and set the cup down with a tiny click. "You have to remember that any deal can fall through, Gordy. You could have bankrupted yourself." She smiled. "It's wonderful that you made out so well. I'm proud of you."

The boy flushed, then smiled.

"So," Shan said, "Mr. Sullivan, having cornered the local market on Prime Grade whiskey, seeks to set his own prices. Interesting."

He glanced at his mate.

"I think we might pay him a visit in any case, Priscilla. I do like to broaden my pool of acquaintances. Shall we see if he's receiving guests this evening?"

"Certainly, Captain."

"That's settled then. Thank you, Gordy. You have access to the oddest information. Five cantra, is it? You're becoming quite wealthy."

"Oh, that was months ago! Now I have seven."

"Do you? You'll have to tell me about it." He held up a hasty palm. "After your grandfather and I have concluded our business. Uncle Dick?"

The old man pushed back his chair and Katy-Rose's heart sank to see the glow in his eyes.

"After you, Johnny Galen. Let's sit out on the porch and have a session of talking."

Auctorial Reflections

WELL, GORDY'S BECOME quite the trader. And here his stepfather was afraid the boy was becoming an idle layabout.

He does seem to have been industrious, as well, during his time as cabin boy on the *Passage*. We're never told, in *Conflict of Honors*, what the cabin boy is paid, but we *are* told that the pet librarian's salary for the last half of the route is one-tenth cantra, plus the lowman share of any crew bonuses. For Gordy to have come home with six cantra...possibly defies belief. Certainly, given New Dublin's probable economy, laying three cantra against whiskey futures seems excessive.

Still, I'm glad he made out so well.

Exchange rates and pay-levels aside, I like this chapter. I like the fact that Shan takes Gordy, and his information, seriously. I like the fact that, while Katy-Rose is rightly horrified that Gordy could have "beggared" the family, her reason is not his age, or supposed inexperience. She might not understand the market, but she doesn't doubt that *Gordy* understands the market. I like the fact that Priscilla is learning how to deadpan answers to Shan's more outrageous flights.

I also want to hear some of the stories Shan has to tell about the times *he* was "sure."

Sharon Lee
May 10, 2015

Chapter the Fifth

Celbridge-on-the Louch
New Dublin

R ichard leaned back and crossed his legs, ankle resting on knee. "You're still wanting to take the boy on, Johnny?"

"More than ever."

"Has a talent for the trading, doesn't he?" Richard was complacent. "Comes from his father, I don't doubt. What a gambler that man was! Only bet he ever lost to my knowledge was the one said he could swim across the louch here." He sighed. "Of course, he was deep in his cups at the time. . . You'll be clearing this with Himself?"

"With Val Con?" Shan shook his head. "It's up to yos'Galan whether or not to take a fosterling into yos'Galan. It might have been necessary to have the delm's permission, if Gordy were from an—unallied—clan. Or if Val Con were delm, instead of nadelm and biding his sweet time."

"That's a likely lad, Johnny; you'd look far and come up with none likelier. But it strikes me that—what is it? twenty Standards?—is a bit young to be taking up as king."

"Twenty-three. And it is, of course. He's twelve years short of full majority. . .yos'Galan will hold the trust as long as needed—I believe Nova was born to administer a clan, Uncle Dick! Details are her passion. Maybe I'll resign and let her run yos'Galan after Val

Con takes the Ring. Though I expect she'd die of boredom, after having run Korval entire. . .Have you seen Val Con recently?"

"He dropped by a time back—just before Gordy was coming home, I think. Said he was on the 'garbage run' and happened to be in the sector. Do you see him often yourself?"

"He's home now. Relumma's leave. . ." He turned his head, and spoke in the local tongue.

"A fine day to you, Housefather."

"And to the guest."

Morgan hesitated in the doorway; glanced to his wife's father.

"I'd be hearing what's decided for the boy. I stand father to him, though he denies it."

The man radiated determination. Shan took a sip of the sweet local wine and held his tongue. The matter was for Uncle Dick to decide.

"We've just been having a bit of family chat," Richard said slowly, "and it's right you are that we should be taking business in hand." He paused. "We'll be speaking Terran, young Morgan. Johnny's hold of our tongue is none so good as that."

Shan privately thought his command of Old Gaelic equal to the task of negotiating Gordy's future with the one person here who seemed aware of the boy as a unique individual and actively wished him well. He sighed gently and took another cloying sip of wine.

"That's very well," Morgan was saying staunchly. "I'll just be getting Katy from her harping for the minute and have her tell me what's being said."

Shan stirred. Get Katy-Rose from her music? He recalled several occasions when summoning Val Con from his music had generated more difficulties than solutions.

"Get Gordy."

Morgan goggled.

"Gordy? Into an adult circle? You'll do well not to encourage such things, Mister Galen. The lad's father took him about to all the story-gathers and smiled if he sassed an elder. It's been thankless, it has, trying to teach him to behave like a fitting boy. And it's been that much worse since he's gone a-trading. Mercy knows how we'll keep him a boy when next he comes home."

"He's barely a boy, now," Shan snapped, "and he'll certainly not be by the time the next trip's done. Time to start teaching him to be an adult!"

Morgan blinked and Richard raised his eyebrows. With a start, Shan realized that he'd spoken in Terran and was about to offer an intelligible apology to the man, when—

"Get Gordy, Morgan," Richard said. "This concerns him more nearly than any. Best he knows the whole of it."

A moment's hesitation, then Morgan was gone. Shan turned to his uncle.

"Forgive me, Uncle Dick. I spoke out of turn."

"You're the lad's fosterfather, aren't you? As far as I can see, Johnny, you've a perfect right to defend him." He leaned over and patted Shan's arm. "Did my heart good to hear it."

GORDY SAT CROSSLEGGED on the floor by his stepfather's chair, round shoulders stiff with importance; eyes shining. Softly, he spoke Gaelic for Morgan; translating, Shan heard with surprised approval, rather than merely summarizing what was said.

"Line yos'Galan agrees to accept Gordon Finn Arbuthnot as a fosterling into the House. We will be responsible for his needs, education, and care, as we are responsible for any other of the Line. He may, of course, visit his true-home often and he may end the fostering at any time and return here."

Shan paused. Gordy murmured another half-dozen words. Stopped.

"It seems in the best interest of the foster child that he be apprenticed onto *Dutiful Passage*. In keeping with this, an apprentice fee of five cantra is offered Line Davis."

Richard coughed in surprise. Morgan jerked upright.

"Here now, Mister Galen! It's not buying the boy you are!"

"He's right, Johnny. We're not hurting for money. It's possible for you to do this as a favor, isn't it? We're kin."

Shan nodded.

"But we're speaking of two different things, Uncle Dick. yos'Galan will have Gordy with joy. As Thodelm, I'm pleased to gain such a son for the House. There's the favor—and it Balances both ways.

"The other matter is one of education. It seems clear to me, in my capacity as Gordy's foster father, that his abilities would best be put to use on a tradeship. Like the *Passage*. It's proper that *the ship* pay an apprentice fee. And it properly goes to the true-family."

Once again, the soft flow of Gaelic continued for a space, then faded. Richard frowned and turned his head to look out over the louch. Morgan looked ready to speak; thought better of it after a glance at his father-in-law's profile. Gordy sat and fairly shone.

Richard turned back.

"Five cantra. How long an apprenticeship does that buy?"

"Ten Standards."

"The lad will be overage when he comes back to us!" Morgan said, disbelieving.

"Not overaged, Housefather," Shan said gently. "Merely adult, by local custom."

"I see," Richard said, drily. "And the lad will earn a wage on the ship and have a chance to find out, would you say, Johnny, if he's apt for the trading?"

"I'd say so, Uncle Dick. Yes."

The older man nodded sharply.

"That's a deal."

He held out a hand.

Shan took it; solemnly shook.

"Done."

Across the room, Gordy let out a shuddering sigh, began to rise.

. .

Shan shook his head, very slightly. Gordy sank back.

"Gordon."

"Yes, Grandad?"

"You've seven cantra of your own?"

"Yes, Grandad."

"If you're willing to put those up, I'll match them and propose this: Of the fourteen, five will go into municipal bonds here, in your name. Six will go, if your foster father is willing, to buy the two of us a share of the *Dutiful Passage's* next voyage. Three will be your own, to do with as you see fit. Do you find that proposal fair?"

A pause.

"No, sir."

Richard's brows went up.

"What's unfair in it?"

"You're putting in seven cantra, but you're only taking profit from three. Can we agree that three cantra of my own money goes into bonds; that we buy a share-and-a-quarter between us, with your contribution seven cantra and mine two? I'll take two cantra investment money."

"That's your notion of fair, is it?"

"Yes, sir."

"It sounds equitable to me, Uncle Dick."

The older man turned his head to glare.

"Rot you, Johnny Galen. You're your father's son and that's no mistake!"

Shan grinned.

After a moment, so did Richard, though reluctantly.

"All right, Gordy, I accept your terms. At the end of this trip, come to me and we'll discuss the possibility of a partnership."

"Thank you, Grandad. . ." It seemed he would say more, then faltered to a stop.

Richard nodded, and rose.

"You be a good boy. Morgan, come with me, lad. We'd best make Katy-Rose understand."

Shan stood and watched them out of the room. Then he smiled and held out his arms.

"All right, Gordy."

Auctorial Reflections

WELL, THERE; THAT WASN't hard, was it?

I'm awfully glad that Morgan was persuaded not to fetch Katy-Rose from her music. The poor woman needs some time with her harp after the last couple days.

We managed to get some Liaden cultural information into this bit—go, us!—such as the age of majority being 35 Standard Years, and remind people of Val Con's ultimate place in the clan, as we've only seen him as the younger brother being dragged around to parties by his sisters. Also, I'm glad to hear that he's not above subverting the Garbage Run to serve his own purposes.

Boy, Morgan doesn't quite Get It, does he? Happily, Shan does. I had to stop and do the math on the proposed deal that closes out the interaction with Richard, and yanno? Gordy's right. His way *is* fairer.

Oh, and for those wondering about the whole "Johnny Galen" thing: John and Sean are the same name. Steve and I pronounce "Shan" as "Sean" (which is to say Shawn-rhymes-with-dawn). Therefore! Shan equates to John, and becomes Johnny, in affection.

Just a joke, that's all. Nothing to see here. Move along.

Sharon Lee
May 17, 2015

Chapter the Sixth

Celbridge-on-the-Louch
New Dublin

"Ms. Mendoza?"

Priscilla glanced up from the portable screen with a smile.

"Yes, Ms. Davis? Is there something I can do for you?"

Katy-Rose hesitated, calloused harper's hands fluttering until she wove the fingers firmly together and held them captive before the buckle of her belt.

"I was wondering if I might as you some questions. Not," she added with a hasty glance at the screen, "if you're busy, of course."

Priscilla laughed softly.

"My lessons. They'll be here later. Unfortunately." She touched a stud and the amber glow faded.

Katy-Rose drifted into the guest room and sat on the edge of the bed.

"Lessons? Are you a scholar?"

The outworld woman laughed again, shaking her head.

"No. I'm studying how to be first mate on the *Passage*. There's a lot to learn."

"I'm sure there must be," murmured Katy-Rose vaguely. She chewed her lip. "I—where do you live, Ms. Mendoza?"

"On Pelthraza Street, in Solcintra."

Priscilla folded her hands atop the portable unit, face serene, watching the dance of the other woman's emotions without attempting, just yet, to calm them.

"Solcintra?" Katy-Rose looked at her sharply. "But you're not—"

"I'm not Liaden, no. I'm originally from Sintia, which is Terran."

"And you studied to be a bard there?"

"A bard?" Priscilla frowned slightly. "I did learn to tell stories as part of my—education. And to chant and recite genealogies." Another brief, bright smile. "Not precisely a bard, I think."

"But near the thought." Katy-Rose decided, and her stress eased somewhat.

"Do you know—my cousin—well?"

"Shan and I are friends," Priscilla said carefully. "But I haven't known him long. Only a few Standard Months. I see him and his family often—Trealla Fantrol is just outside of Solcintra. Anthora comes by almost daily. . ."

"The youngest sister," Katy-Rose reminded herself, nodding. "A pretty little thing, I remember. . .Shan himself is not—married—at this time?"

Priscilla blinked.

"No. . ."

Relief zapped through the other's pattern.

"Well, thank Mercy for that! I think contract-marriage is—is barbaric! And that poor little girl, all alone in that huge house, with no mother—"

"Padi?"

Priscilla nearly laughed again, caught it and controlled it.

"I've never seen a child more spoiled! Both of her aunts are there, and a nurse, and Shan and Val Con—she wears them all on her finger!"

"Yes, but Shan isn't home often. And Val Con even less..."

She shook her head, obstinate.

"It doesn't seem right. Do you know, I don't even know the name of the child's mother? She lived in that house for a year, gave birth and vanished. It's unnatural. . ." She paused. "Will Gordy have to contract-wed?"

"He's a bit young for that, surely?"

Katy-Rose was not soothed.

"Who knows what a Liaden will take it into his head to do? Here's Shan not yet a man and sold off to some clan of another and living there until the woman had her child and then here he comes home again. I asked him a visit or two gone by how his son went on and I'll swear to you he didn't know what I asked him!"

"What did he say?" asked Priscilla, paying out a length of calm to the woman.

"Why that he heard the child prospered!"

"Then no doubt he does."

Priscilla strengthened the bond between them, added comfort, seeking to create a clear space in the storm of the other's grief and confusion.

"Shan is not a careless person, but it's not his responsibility to care for the child of another clan. He loves his daughter very well—and his sisters and foster brother, too!"

"He doesn't mean to be unkind, I know," Katy-Rose acknowledged. "But he's very—odd, isn't he?"

"Gordy loves him," suggested Priscilla softly, and Katy-Rose nodded.

"That's true. And he manages the boy wonderfully well, doesn't he? He doesn't raise his voice or threaten and yet there's Gordy running for wine and as good as I haven't seen him since—since Morgan and I. . ."

"It's difficult, sometimes, to love people as they are and not as you'd like them to be."

Calm was won. Priscilla worked to expand it; to slay the mother-fears and the guilt; to shore up the sagging lines of affection.

"Gordy shows talent for trading. He has flexibility and intelligence. Why shouldn't he be trained? Especially since he has the desire, too."

"Why shouldn't he, indeed?" Katy-Rose smiled suddenly, and Priscilla sealed her work into place. "It's a good thing I came and spoke with you, Ms. Mendoza. I feel a great deal better now."

"I'm glad," murmured Priscilla, disengaging and leaning back in her chair.

Katy-Rose stood; leaned over to touch Priscilla's folded hands.

"You're a good woman. Gordy told me what you did for him. And I can see it in you, like a good, strong flame. You'll take care of my lad, won't you? Maybe even teach him some of the songs?"

"My songs aren't the same as yours. . ."

"No matter," said Katy-Rose, turning to leave. "They're likely no different in the ways that count."

Auctorial Reflections

IT SEEMS LIKE PRISCILLA's done something rather more than a simple calming down of rattled nerves here, most especially given the last line. I'm not sure that Hestya would approve.

Katy-Rose had come to Priscilla, after all, partly because she was afraid of what partaking of Liaden custom—which is *so different* from New Dublin custom—might do to her little boy. Then she allows that Priscilla's songs are likely no different, at heart, than Katy-Rose's own songs. That's a little. . .disturbing. Or, it's hardcore Terran-centric.

I think I want to know where Priscilla got the stud, and when she has to give him back. On the other hand—no, maybe I don't actually want to know that.

So, hey! The first mention of Padi yos'Galan, who has kept her name All This Time, even unto *Ghost Ship*, where she has a speaking role, and *Alliance of Equals*! where she has—somewhat more.

Otherwise: culture notes! Contract marriage! Anthora in a cameo role as a "pretty little thing." And we never did solve the issue of whether Gordy will be compelled to contract-wed, which is to say, will he ultimately identify as Liaden, or Terran? Those of us who have written and read ahead in the series know that this choice, at least, has lately become much less difficult for him, if, indeed, he ever saw the choice or perceived it as difficult.

It's not a particularly well-written chapter, but it gets the work done, I guess. Definitely building the story scene-by-scene, which is a perfectly acceptable way to do the thing, but, honest, a scene can do more than one job.

Sharon Lee
May 19, 2015

Chapter the Seventh

Celbridge-on-the-Louch
New Dublin

They rounded the corner into Farmingham Crescent and the
breeze off the louch slapped their faces.

Beside her, Shan shivered and sealed the front of his jacket. She
slid her arm through his.

"Cold?"

"Damp. Why do you suppose they chose to stockpile water
just here, Priscilla? It's very picturesque, of course, but consider the
townspeople. Cold and damp. Damp and cold. Dreary."

"You thought it looked very nice this afternoon."

"Sunlight lends a certain charm. Is it over-optimistic to hope
that Mr. Sullivan has something drinkable in his cellar?"

She laughed softly and drew an unconscious few inches closer
to his side.

"I think your choice is between good ale and bad wine. Or
maybe whiskey."

"Do you think he'll offer samples of the goods? That would be
pleasant. . .Three cantra to seven in half a local year! We may have
bitten off more than we can decently swallow, Priscilla. How do
you find your son, now?"

"Much improved from our first meeting." She sighed. "I'm afraid the situation would have come to blows very soon, my friend."

"We have, in fact, performed a rescue. I'd surmised that from Uncle Dick's message. One does wish that he would have been a bit more specific, however. The fact is, Priscilla, neither Katy-Rose or Morgan see Gordy as anything approaching adult. And he's unfolding to halfling before their eyes!"

"Katy-Rose wanted to know if Gordy would be made to contract-wed," Priscilla offered. "She was very concerned about the possibility. She said she thinks contract-marriages are barbaric."

"Well," Shan said drily; "she's right about that."

There was a short silence.

"It would be a very distance alliance with Korval—and he's full Terran, raised to Terran ways. I don't doubt there would be some to try it, but—Oh, ye gods and goddesses!"

He was abruptly still, a slim, silver-topped tree growing by the shore of the louch.

"What?"

She dropped his arm, senses wide, scanning. . .His pattern was a flickering play of amused horror, fondness, and resignation.

"Shan?"

He laughed a little and touched her hair.

"It's nothing, my friend. I was only remembering when Val Con came halfling. Sheerest luck that either of us lived through it, never mind both. My father couldn't have known. . .I came halfling and Healer between one heartbeat and the next. Spent my first months in the Healer's Hall, leaning control, technique. . .They threw in bed-lessons and a few basic adult-rules as a kindness. . .We'll have our hands full, I think, Priscilla."

She wanted to grab the hand on her hair, push her face into his warm palm, taste it with lips and tongue; hold him tight; join mouths; stroke the thick white hair—

"Priscilla."

Carefully, she moved out from under his hand. Drew a breath. Another. Began the sequence to enclosed passion.

And only then perceived the tendril of calm he offered.

She fell into it; shrouded herself in it; breathed it into her.

"Goddess bless you, my dear."

"Always of service."

Concern/compassion/guilt/love/lust radiated faintly through his control matrix. He stood quite still, hands loose at his sides.

"I'm sorry, Shan."

Flaring outbreak of passion.

"Do you think I don't go through it, too? That I don't ache to hold you? Weep to kiss you? If it weren't so necessary, I'd—"

He glanced around at the swelling louch, and damp grass, and offered her a ragged moonlit grin.

"Well, perhaps not *this instant*."

She laughed softly; straightened, wearing his calm like the cloak of a queen.

"We'll be keeping Mr. Sullivan waiting."

"That won't do, will it?" he responded with the same brittle lightness.

Without another word, they turned and continued on their way, Shan's hands in his jacket pockets and a stranger's distance between them

AS IT TURNED OUT, MR. Sullivan kept them waiting. The well-fed individual who escorted them to the lounge imparted the intelligence that, "Mr. S'll be with you shortly. Please make yourselves comfortable."

No refreshment was offered.

Shan perched on the side arm of a recliner. Priscilla prowled the room's perimeter.

It was a room of many parts. One part was the long end wall, lined with tape-crammed shelves. No bound books, and little fiction. In the realm of non-fiction, however, Mr. Sullivan's tastes were catholic. Priscilla continued her prowl.

The aquarium was given careful scrutiny, Shan noted, but the spindly table with the reading screen perched precariously atop hardly earned a glance. She frowned into the curio cabinet, but the glare of light off dusty glass panels apparently defeated her. She skirted the bar and a cluster of clean-topped occasional tables with no more than a cursory inspection.

And so came to the tapestry.

Priscilla halted, face arrested.

She stepped forward and fingered the piece; inspected the reverse side; bent over the dark red and yellow pattern as if looking for some identification.

"Something?" he inquired, strolling over to join her.

She thrust a corner into his hand.

"This is fine work. Done by hand. See that tying off of the yellow there? And here, where the weaver had to go back and work over the section? I wonder if it's local."

He studied it, noting the things she pointed out and others, learned from his own experience trading cloth.

"I didn't know you were an expert on textiles, Priscilla."

She looked startled.

"House Mendoza's fortune comes from textiles," she said hesitantly. "I was taken around to the mills and to the weavers almost before I could walk. I continued to study, even after I was—taken into Circle—for training. I had my own loom. . ." She touched a blazing yellow flower at the tapestry's heart.

"It was too big to bring away."

Around a swell of pity, he began, "Priscilla. . ."

And their host was with them.

Mike Sullivan was a burly Terran, red-cheeked and smiling. A full reddish beard drew the eye away from a freckled, hairless scalp.

"Captain yos'Galan. Ms. Mendoza. Good of you to come, gentles. I appreciate how important your time is and I apologize for keeping you cooling your heels."

He paused, brown eyes shrewd.

"Good piece of work, eh? Picked that up on Filmore, in Mega Sirse System."

"Oh." Priscilla smiled at him. "I was hoping it was local."

"No such luck, eh? You traders can't have all the breaks. Would you like something to drink? Captain? Care to taste before we talk?"

"An excellent idea?"

"Ms. Mendoza?"

"Thank you, yes."

A few moments later, satisfactorily provided with refreshment, they sat in wide Terran chairs and raised glasses in polite salute to Sullivan's proposed, "To profitable dealing!"

"For all," Shan added with a smile, and tasted the contents of his glass.

Priscilla took a careful sip and found the stuff unexpectedly smooth: the fire ignited in the stomach, not the throat.

"Mighty fine, eh?"

Sullivan was beaming, certain their judgment would match his. Priscilla kept her face noncommittal.

Shan shrugged.

"Adequate."

Sullivan laughed indulgently.

"You traders are a cagey bunch. Now, I like a trade where everything comes out of the pockets and onto the tabletop where we can all touch and see. My proposed price for a wooden keg of Prime Grade whiskey, just like we're drinking now, based on a shipment of no less than two hundred barrels, is ninety-eight bits per. Fair?"

Shan leaned back in his chair and took another appreciative sip of whiskey. His light eyes roamed the room; rested on the red-and-yellow tapestry.

"Beautiful work. Filmore, did you say?"

"That's right."

Sullivan frowned.

Shan nodded, eyes still dreaming on the colors.

"My dreadful memory. . .Do correct me if i I'm wrong, Mr. Sullivan, but—Mega Sirse System. That's controlled by the Juntavas, is it not?"

Priscilla stiffened slightly. Juntavas?

Sullivan was nodding affably.

"So it is. I do a favor from time to time—"

"And the cornering of the local market in Prime grade whiskey is part of a—favor—you owe the Juntavas?"

"Captain. . ."

The big man waved a soothing hand, his pattern radiating no distress at all.

"It's a fair price. What difference does it make it to you who's behind the deal?"

Shan sighed; leaned forward and set the glass aside.

"Do forgive me, sir. I am of Clan Korval. Our understanding with the Juntavas is—and has been for many years—that we do not touch theirs and they do not touch ours. It's been an exemplary arrangement. You understand that I hesitate to alter it."

"I see." Sullivan stroked his beard. "I owe you an apology, Captain. It didn't occur to me to check your clan affiliation. Foolish. I appreciate your forbearance."

"No forbearance, sir. I'm glad that we understand each other. Such fine whiskey—you should have no trouble placing it elsewhere."

"It'll just take a little longer."

Mike Sullivan paused.

"Allow me to send you a keg of the finest for your own use. As a personal gift from me to you."

Shan rose and bowed gently.

"Perhaps not." He smiled. "Please do believe me, Mr. Sullivan. No offense has been taken. A fair evening to you."

"And to you," the big man responded, rising ponderously.

The doorway was abruptly full of the overfed doorman. Shan bowed again, gathered Priscilla with a glance and followed the man out.

Auctorial Reflections

THERE MUST'VE BEEN a sale on sentence fragments down at the used word store the day we wrote this chapter.

Well, let's see. . .I find myself not in agreement with Shan touching Priscilla's hair, despite the fact that the Priscilla and Shan line was intended to be more along the lines of science fiction romance, as we call it today.

I'm also displeased with this shrouding tendril.

On the other hand, I very much *like* Shan agreeing with his cousin's assessment of contract-marriage, while he immediately starts to do the marriage mart math in his head—well, after all, who would want the boy—and why? And would such an alliance profit Korval?

Mike Sullivan may possibly have forgotten to "check" Shan's "clan affiliation," though I'm betting it's common knowledge among folk there in the town that the Davis family has Liaden kin, yes, it does. Who, you ask? Why, none other than Tree-and-Dragon itself!

I'm leaning toward this little encounter having been a test of Shan's. . .integrity, let's say. The Juntavas isn't above putting out feelers, after all.

And I will note here that, despite it all, Mike Sullivan did *not* play Shan for a tourist, having offered a starting price under one hundred bits the keg.

I had forgotten that, about House Mendoza having made its money in textiles. And I'd *completely* forgotten that Priscilla had her own loom, even as an initiate in Circle House.

REMINDER: There will be no (that's **NO**) new chapter posted on Monday June 8, because—book tour. Look for Chapter Eight on Monday, June 15.

Sharon Lee

May 27, 2015

Chapter the Eighth

Trealla Fantrol
Liad

Gordy was lost.

Well, you couldn't *precisely* call it 'lost'. Not with housecomms stationed here and there throughout the rooms he'd already explored. If he kept going, he'd probably find another one and then he could call in and whoever answered would dispatch someone of this vast household to escort him back to known territory.

But he sure would like to find his *own* way back.

This room gave onto a hallway: wood paneled walls and uncarpeted floors. Left or right?

Gordy chose left.

His soft houseboots made no sound on the plain floor, which pleased him.

Almost as quiet as Val Con.

It ocurred to him that he might study to become a Scout himself and he scrutinized the idea intensely for three minutes before putting it aside without regret.

I'm going to be a Trader.

That thought felt solid, like the Tree Priscilla had taught him. So, it was decided.

The hallway curved slightly and ended abruptly at a blank wooden door. Gordy had a moment of hope, quickly dashed. If it were an outside door—but no. The green glass knob set in the center testified that this was an older portion of the house. Trealla Fantrol had grown in a spiral, so that the further in you went, the older the house got. Which meant. . .

Gordy sighed around a lively flash of irritation—*stupid house*—and turned the knob.

Silvery bars, trampoline, tumbling mats, springboards, hurdles, one pair of rings suspended from the ceiling; another attached to the wall. . .

"A gym."

Gordy walked slowly forward, turning around several times to make sure he saw everything. He paused by the side of the trampoline, sorely tempted.

"Housecomm," he told himself sternly, and continued, though not without a pang.

There were three ping-pong tables at the back of the room, paddles and balls slung in a net bag hanging beneath each. Over to the far left, the wall was marked with squares, circles and triangles—targets, Gordy guessed. The floor was broken up into rectangles; four of them, each separated by a strip of colored tile.

There was no housecomm.

There was, however, a door in the back right corner, its center-knob brilliant blue.

Gordy went through.

And stopped, blinking in the reflected sunlight; gasping sodden air into startled lungs—

It was as big as Louch Skerrie, back home. The room was hot, hotter than it ever got at home, and Liaden sunlight poured like the finest yellow butter through the glass roof straight into the smooth aquamarine waters. There were plants, too, Gordy saw through his dazzle, stretching greedily upward. . .

"Well met, Cousin!"

Gordy blinked again; walked carefully toward the expanse of water, houseboots shuffing against the baked red tiles.

"Have you come for a swim?" the pool asked him.

Gordy squinted; made out a sleek dark head, and elbows resting on the pool edge.

"Val Con?"

"Ah, I apologize. Shall I opaque the window?"

"No, that's OK. My eyes are getting used to it. It's just that the halls and stuff are pretty dim. Compared to this."

He came to what he considered a safe distance from the water, and took a careful cross-legged seat on the floor.

"Have you come to swim?" Val Con asked him again.

"I don't know how to swim," Gordy explained. "I'm lost."

"An easy condition to attain, in Trealla Fantrol. At least on the *Passage* one knows that a place is either on the horizontal or the vertical and can locate it from there by the application of logic. Trealla Fantrol requires intuition, skill, and not a little luck."

Gordy laughed.

"I guess I should have asked somebody to take me on a tour, but I was pretty sure I could figure it out by myself."

"The tour should have been offered, I think," Val Con commented in his soft, accented Terran. "Have you been lost very long?"

The boy shrugged.

"Couple hours, maybe. Saw some housecomms, but I kept thinking I'd come to an outside door *soon*. . ."

He paused, considering the face before him.

"Grandad says. . ." he began, and then blurted—"*Are* you a king?"

One eyebrow slid upward.

"No, a Scout. Are *you* a king?"

"Me?" He groggled; shook his head. "Not me. I'm just Gordy."

"An entirely satisfactory thing to be. Why do you not swim?"

"I told you, I can't. I—Ma wouldn't let me learn, see, because Da—my father—drowned in the louch."

"All the more reason for you to learn," Val Con commented. He tipped his head. "I would be pleased to teach you."

Gordy squirmed.

"That's OK. . .I mean—I'll think about it, thanks."

"No thanks owed. The teaching would grant me joy."

Val Con put his palms flat on the floor and pushed. He popped out of the water like a cork, water sheeting off of him.

"If you can wait a moment or two, Cousin, while I dry and dress, we might walk back to the family rooms together."

He padded off without waiting for an answer.

Auctorial Reflections

VAL CON SAYS, "I APOLOGIZE."

Also, I had forgotten the bit about Trealla Fantrol having been built in a spiral. I don't think we ever mention that detail again, though we do say that the house is easy to get lost in, if you haven't been given "the tour."

That said, does it make *perfect* sense to put the gym and the pool in the most protected area of the house?

The scene itself is well enough, but rather thin. In fact, I'm finding it interesting from a "how we do it" standpoint to read these chapters and note what we'd do on the next pass, and the next—partial passes of this particular scene, which we do on the fly—adding in layers and creating depth. This is one of the reason it takes us "so long" to write a book: we usually lay in the skeleton scene, then Add Stuff as it occurs to us—some the next day, when we review the work from the day before; some when we're further along in the book, and A Detail—or, yanno, A Subplot—occurs to us. It's something we do almost without thinking about it, in this age of computers, but it still takes time.

Sharon Lee

June 12, 2015

Chapter the Ninth

Trealla Fantrol

Liad

Indisputably, the glass was moving.

Not, it was true, quickly, or even very much.

But it *was* moving.

Val Con sighed gently and spared a moment of his attention to rectify the situation. . .

"There! You see how he does it!" Anthora was practically singing in jubilation.

"Inertia. . ." murmured Priscilla Mendoza.

Val Con sighed once more and turned.

Anthora was sitting by the window, holding her own glass in firm small fingers. Priscilla, who was staying for dinner, stood nearer him—perhaps four feet away. Her face held an expression of puzzled intentness he found altogether charming.

"It's a great deal like your Tree thing, Priscilla, isn't it? Except he's doing it to something *else*, rather than to himself—"

Val Con drifted close to the Terran woman; smiled with a calculated upsweep of lashes.

"I do other tricks," he murmured.

She laughed, black eyes dancing.

"Which you are completely uninterested in displaying."

"Interested," he corrected gently, "but without hope."

179

"Val Con, stop flirting with Priscilla," Anthora directed from her chair. "Tell her how you stopped the wineglass. It's not *rooted*, Priscilla—and he's not doing anything to it *now*. But, I can't move it a hair's breadth."

"I don't want you to move it a hair's breadth," her brother informed her, with heat. "I want you to leave it alone."

Anthora regarded him with dignity.

"This is an experiment."

"Experiment on Shan."

"Shan's a Healer, not a *dramliza*."

"Nor am I a wizard. I'm merely a man who wants his wineglass left in peace."

"Now, brother, don't be ill-tempered," she cajoled. "It's a remarkable sort of thing to be able to do, and I found I couldn't explain it to Priscilla, so naturally I had to show her. And you *are* a wizard, *denubia*. Only a wizard could do what you're doing—or not doing, now. Isn't that right, Priscilla?"

"Perhaps."

She had turned that look of absent intensity full upon him. He experienced a thrill of warmth and an extended tickling sensation, as if one of his cats had brushed against his naked soul.

"You felt that," Priscilla said; it was not a question.

"Yes; and I wish you will not do it again."

She inclined her head.

"It was not my intention to hurt you. Forgive me."

"Ah." He extended a slim golden hand and touched her sleeve. "You did not hurt me, friend. On the contrary, it was rather pleasant. It's the training, I think. Scouts are not to be taken unaware."

"I see," she murmured, and it seemed to him that she did. "I only wanted to know if you were in fact what Anthora calls a wizard."

"And you find that I am a very poor wizard, indeed, beside which I am empathic, yet not an empath." He moved his shoulders. She smiled.

"Not all wizardry involves lifting wine glasses and lighting fires. There's something. . ."

But what that something was he did not then learn. The door to the gather-room slid open and they turned, expecting Shan and Nova, finally freed of their meeting with Delm Hasla and Mr. dea'Gauss.

Gordy stepped into the room, door sighing behind him. He looked uncomfortable in his new blue tunic, but his face lit when he saw Priscilla.

"Hello, Gordy. Ready for the *Passage*?" She smiled and put a hand on his shoulder. He beamed.

"I sure am!" A candle's worth of light left his eyes. "But Shan says I'm going to be Ken Rik's assistant this trip!"

"Ken Rik's not so bad," Priscilla said. "And one of the best ways to learn about trade is by studying the cargo."

"I guess. . ." He was suddenly serious. "Val Con?"

"Yes."

"I—umm—I thought over what you said—and you're right! And. . .I'd like you to teach me how to swim. Please."

"Ah."

He smiled and dared to touch the young cheek.

"I am glad. Let us go."

Turning, he swept the others a bow.

"Priscilla. Sister. I regret. A previous commitment."

Gordy was staring at him in dismay.

"*Now?*"

"There is time for a lesson before the meal. Determination should not be kept waiting."

He started toward the door; glanced back.

"Gordy?"

The boy cast a wild glance at Priscilla, who nodded.

"Go ahead, Gordy. We'll see you at Prime."

"I love to swim before eating," Anthora chimed in; "everything tastes so *good,* afterward."

"Oh," he said, breathlessly; then, "OK."

He took a breath deep enough to lift his stiff shoulders and walked to Val Con, waiting at the door.

"Let's go," he said.

Upon consideration, Val Con did not offer his hand.

GORDY TOOK HIS CLOTHES off and carefully hung them up. Then he sat down, because his knees were shaking. It wouldn't do for Val Con to see he was scared.

He thought wistfully of the Tree. Priscilla had taught him the Tree and it made him strong. Too bad he didn't know anything to make him brave. Maybe he'd ask her, later. There might be something.

Meanwhile, time was passing and Prime was getting closer. If he stayed in the undressing room much longer, Val Con would know he was afraid, anyway.

Gordy sighed, and thought about his Tree for the sheer comfort the mind-picture brought him, and got up. He stared at himself in the mirror: A fair-haired boy with a round beige face and wide-opened brown eyes; his waist soft and his legs sturdy. His cock was scrunched up tight, and he sighed, thinking of Val Con, and Shan, and even Morgan.

Nice to be grown up and not afraid of anything.

But Shan had told Morgan, and Grandpa, that Gordy was growing up. Maybe if he *pretended* not to be scared. . .it would come to be true.

Jaw clamped, Gordy opened the door and went out to the pool to find Val Con.

THE DARK-HAIRED MAN turned from the housecomm with a smile.

"Ready? Come over to the side of the pool. The water's very pretty, isn't it?"

Gordy blinked and looked down. The pool was a calm, lucent azure, reflecting the twilit sky above.

"It is pretty," he said, somewhat surprised.

"And it feels good," Val Con continued, kneeling and slipping his hand beneath the surface.

Gordy did the same, awkwardly. The water was as smooth as old silk, and pleasantly cool.

"Now," murmured the man, "you must learn and always remember this thing: Water is your friend. It does not want you to drown. In fact, water will allow you to rest when you are tired of swimming, so that you may swim again. If you mistrust it, or fight it, or fear it, it will not help you. But if you treat it as a valued friend and ally, then you are safe."

He paused.

"People float. Even if you should fall into the water accidentally, you will rise to the surface. Like this."

He was gone, and there was an explosive *splash*! that didn't quite mask Gordy's cry of, "No!"—and he could see Val Con's dark head, far away down at the bottom of the pool, and he thought about the comm, took a step, and—paused.

Val Con was limp in the water; arms and legs dangling. And yet—he was rising, slowly, inevitably. Gordy stood at the edge of the pool and watched. The sleek head broke water and the man twisted lazily onto his back, where he floated for half-a-dozen heartbeats before righting himself and treading water.

He grinned. "You see?"

Gordy nodded.

"Good. Now, you try."

He went winter-cold in the summery room and it was hard to breathe and his legs were made out of rubber and of stone—

"Gordy." Val Con's voice was firm. "*Denubia*, I swear it; you will come to no harm. Fill your lungs, hold the air in, and jump."

It was impossible.

Gordy felt tears prickling his eyes, and his ears rang. Distantly, he thought of his Tree; closed his eyes to better visualize it; pushed his cheek against the rough bark. He took a deep breath, swallowing the fresh green scent.

Eyes still closed—he jumped.

He nearly yelled when he smacked into the water, but some instinct kept his mouth tight. His eyes did fly open, to a bewildering spangle of bubbles and a distorted—something—on the edge of his watery vision, keeping pace with his descent.

He touched the bottom of the pool and panic nearly won. He'd come such a long way! All that water on top of him! His chest was tight—there was no air! He almost flailed out, but the memory of Val Con, limp and unresisting, rising effortlessly to the surface, interfered with panic, and he deliberately made himself limp, closing his eyes again, and hugging his Tree inside.

Rising was more pleasant than sinking. The water moved by at a less frenzied pace, almost caressing.

Gordy's head broke water. He raised his face, and gulped down a mouthful of air, before clumsily imitating Val Con's supple roll onto his back.

"My feet keep sinking."

"You must be relaxed. Think of how it was when you rose." Val Con's voice was right in his ear.

Gordy turned his head and earned a mouthful of water for the effort. He coughed and began to sink in earnest as a pair of strong arms came under his back, holding him effortlessly above water.

"You will please not drink the contents of the swimming pool." He managed a feeble grin.

"OK."

He stared up at the glassed-out sky, and his grin grew wider.

"Val Con?"

"Yes."

"I did it, didn't I?"

"Indeed you did," Val Con murmured in his ear. "And well. Shall we continue? There is time to teach all of you to float properly before we must go to Prime."

"All right," said Gordy, smiled at the sky.

Auctorial Reflections

WELL, I LIKE THIS BIT. I like the wine glass experiment, and the in-family squabble, and Priscilla laughing. I *really* like Val Con taking Gordy up on his decision before he could change his mind.

And I also like that Val Con *didn't* just pitch the kid into the pool, but had him affirm his decision at every step, and so become steadier in his resolve. That's an important thing. So, brava, Val Con.

I'm wondering when sliding spaceship-like doors were installed at Trealla Fantrol; it's an old house, after all, though not as old as Jelaza Kazone, but perhaps there's been a new wing added.

Someone had commented last week that Gordy, in his wanderings, could have just as easily spoken and Jeeves would have sent someone to find him. The chapters we're exploring were written before Jeeves presented himself to the authors' attention. So you see that it's a fortunate thing that this book was never published, or completed. Had it been, it would have changed the whole universe.

Sharon Lee
June 20, 2015

Chapter the Tenth

Trealla Fantrol
Liad

L ate. And there was work to be done—more than a little, with the *Passage* due to leave Liad in four local days. Shan flung his cloak across the carved wood arm of an antique hall chair. It was his own fault, of course. Seeing Priscilla home to Pelthraza Street should have taken no more than an hour. Yet the hour had grown somehow into two...three...approaching four.

You see her daily, he scolded himself. *How can you have so much to talk about?*

But Priscilla hadn't seemed bored. Gods knew he'd be with her still, if the Universe were ordered exactly as Shan yos'Galan wished it...

Work, he reminded himself.

He ducked into the gather-room and poured himself a glass of *misravot*. The room, like the hall, was faintly illuminated by night-dims. The rest of the family must be abed, then. Sighing, Shan headed for the stairway and his rooms.

Paused, head cocked. Very faintly, he discerned music. Omnichora music.

Someone was awake.

Shan hesitated, the pile of invoices and last-minute emergencies seeming all at once soothing.

If it's not tonight, it will have to be tomorrow, he told himself sternly. *And Nova specifically asked you to speak with him.*

He stood in the darkened hall a few moments longer, sipping his wine and listening to the faint, undistinguished notes. Then, with a sense of imminent dismay, he turned and followed the music.

SHAN PAUSED OUTSIDE the door to the music room. The notes had altered somewhat during his stroll down the halls. They were stronger; balanced and precise, as if someone elses had taken the original player's place at the 'chora.

The sound faded.

Shan stepped forward and the door slid open just as the towering opening of "Tocata and Fugue in D Minor" crahsed into being.

Breath caught in his throat. This had been his mother's favorite piece—he had not heard it since her death. Certainly, he had not heard it like this, as if she herself were playing. His vision blurred and it was not Val Con at the 'chora, but Anne Davis, strong and controlled, and—alive—in the music. . .

Painfully, he forced air into tight lungs; ran a quick sequence to bring emotion under control, as if he were about to embark upon a particularly difficult Healing. Pulling out a handkerchief, he gently wiped his cheeks.

He found a chair near the omnichora and sat composed in the dimness, sipping wine and awaiting the end of the music.

It came, as it must, and Val Con turned, hitching one knee up on the bench. In the bluish glow of the keyboard, his face shone wet.

"Well played, Brother," Shan said quietly, and bent forward, offering the glass. "Will you drink?"

"My thanks," Val Con's voice was husky with expended effort. He drank rather more deeply than *misravot* demanded and sighed.

"You're up late," he said, shaking his hair out of his eyes.

"I might say the same of you," Shan pointed out. "However, the luck has served us both. Our sister asked me to speak with you and, since the *Passage* leaves orbit within the half-week, I was a bit puzzled as to how I was to get onto your busy calendar."

"Oh, fluff!" Val Con laughed. "You know as well as I do that you'd only walk in on me some morning while I was still abed—"

"And run the risk of seeing gods-only-know-what? Or—worse!—whom? Hardly. Are you going to drink the whole glass or may I have a sip?"

"Forgive me," Val Con murmured. He took another outrageous swallow and handed the glass back, wine much diminished. "I'd thought you'd be spending the night with Priscilla. . ."

Shan froze.

"Priscilla and I are not pleasure-loves."

"That much is obvious," Val Con said irritably. "What I cannot for my heart understand, Brother, is *why* you are not!"

He leaned forward abruptly.

"By the gods—Shan, you are a Healer! Can you not see the woman loves you?"

"Enough!" The High Tongue, Elder to Junior. "I do not discuss this with you."

"Your first mate," his *cha'leket* swept on, as if he hadn't spoken. "And you return the regard—do you think I don't see? Who accompanies Elsa lo'Retha these past weeks? Traya Maandoln, though she buys the privilege dearly. Rumor is that Shan yos'Galan has given *nubiath'a* and is seen always with the Terran thodelm—"

"I have said—"

"That you do not discuss the matter with me—your word is good!" Val Con snapped. "Tell me-without discussion—what it is you do? The tension between you—how will you run the *Passage* when the captain is ill with wanting the first mate and the first mate desperate for the captain—and neither will aid the other! It's madness."

"Are you telling me how to run my ship?" Shan demanded.

"I'm telling you how to run your life!" Val Con cried.

"Of all—" Outrage and humor warred. Curiosity trumped both. "By what right?"

"By right of being nadelm—Korval-to-be. You endanger yourself and the *Passage*. I require an explanation."

"Right of nadelm, is it? If you're so anxious to throw your weight around, take the damned Ring and get it off my back!"

"Nova serves as *eldema-pernardi*, not you."

"And who is *your heir*, in the event you're hit by space-travelling rocks, or speared by unfriendly savages? Do you think *I* want to be Korval?"

"Brother. . ." Val Con was off the bench, fingertips brushing Shan's cheek, jawline, brow. "Shan?"

He closed his eyes, seeking to marshal his rag-tag resources. Healer, indeed. Opening his eyes, he touched his brother's thin golden cheek.

"*Denubia*, what are we quarreling about?"

"I am not certain," Val Con's face was troubled. "Can you tell me why you have not resolved the thing between you and Priscilla? I ask it, Brother."

Shan sighed deeply.

"*Melant'i*. Priscilla is a stranger to the *Pasasge*; new to the rank. I think—I am certain!—she will be an excellent officer. But it must be proved. By action. Over time. I would not have it. . .rumored. . .that she gained the post through the captain's bed. I would not have Priscilla hear it and perhaps believe it—as she might. There must be no doubt of the first mate. We agreed to set pleasure aside until she had established her *melant'i* more fully." He shrugged.

"And so you put yourself under this strain before even the ship leaves orbit—"

Shan straightened.

"Priscilla is a Healer, too. We can scan each other's pattern for comfort and companionship. . .It's difficult to explain, *denubia*. Suffice to say that it's not as bad as it could be."

"I take your word on it." Val Con shifted slightly. "What was it Nova asked you to say to me?"

Oh, gods; after this? Still, it would not be more palatable in daylight. Shan swallowed *misravot* without tasting it, and set the glass aside.

"The First-Speaker-in-Trust asked me to say to you that she will be pleased to sanction a contract-marriage between yourself and any suitable lady of your choice. She—"

"No."

Utter rejection, slamming down so hard Shan's outer ears rang with the force of it.

He extended a hand.

"Any lady you chose, Brother. Korval-in-Trust has said it. Surely, on all of Liad, there is *one* lady you find possible."

"No."

Val Con retreated a step. . .two—and abruptly sat on the edge of the music bench, his eyes in shadow.

"You must provide the clan with your heir. It is your duty no less than the duty of us all. Why not get it over with quickly? One consolation is that you're unlikely to be contracted to provide a child for another clan. . ."

Val Con said nothing.

"Is your heart engaged?"

He asked the question as gently as he could; then, more sharply, as the impossibility of such a match struck him: "You're not in love with Nova, are you, *denubia*?"

Gods, he probably was. They were of an age; growing up in each other's pockets. And the relationship was too close to risk a child; Petrella yos'Galan and Sella yos'Phelium had been twins. . .

"Nova is my sister," Val Con said flatly, and Shan read affection and kin-love and a stirring of sorrow, but nothing more. He swallowed relief.

"Then there's nothing to hold you back from seeking out a congenial lady—"

"No!"

Val Con was on his feet, quiet voice rising shockingly.

"I will not! I—I *can*not!"

"Can't? What do you mean, *can't*? You've had lovers; a contract-marriage is a little less and a little more than an affair of pleasure—but it's certainly not a lifemating. A year—two at the longest—and you're out of it—"

"No. Brother, I swear to you; it is not possible. I—Would I grieve my family—and risk Nova's temper!—if it were possible to buy peace—so easily?" He flung his hands out, palms up in supplication.

"Shan, I *cannot*."

He believed it; his pattern confirmed it. Shan bowed his head.

"So be it, then. But don't expect the First Speaker to believe it."

"She does not. Else why would she send you to speak with me when only this noon she and I spoke on the subject?"

"Now, that she did not tell me!"

Shan laughed in frustration, as down the hall a mechanical bird sang the very early morning hour.

"Ah, blast it all. No sleep tonight. Or do I mean last night?"

"Who can tell?" murmured Val Con, linking arms and turning him toward the door.

"Allow me to walk you to your rooms, Brother."

They went down the hall and up the stairs; two slim shadows, one tall and silver-haired; the other small and dark and utterly silent. At Shan's door, the smaller stretched to kiss the taller on the lips.

"Sleep well, Shan-brother."

"Sleep well, *denubia*."

He laid a light hand on the other's arm.

"If you happen to find out *why* you 'can't,' let me know, all right?"

"Yes," Val Con agreed, and went silently down the hall toward his rooms.

Auctorial Reflections

IN *Conflict of Honors*, Er Thom has been dead for three Standards. Anne died about a Standard before that, in an unspecified "accident." The survivors are clearly still adjusting to their losses, and to their various new *melant'is*. Granted, Val Con has been "nadelm" for his entire life—though, if I were writing this now, I'd probably be on the search for a Liaden word or phrase that means something like "Delm Intended," or perhaps just the more recently-invented "Delm Genetic," because he is very much more than the nadelm, i.e. the current delm's eventual replacement. Val Con *is* Korval, he became so when the previous delm "died." Had Daav died without issue, Er Thom would have become delm, as the previous delm's heir. But Val Con exists, merely too young to take up his duties, which Er Thom takes up, in trust, and for the good of the clan.

But, now, Uncle Er Thom is gone, and the only two clanmembers of the older generation who are left are Kareen yos'Phelium, and Luken bel'Tarda. And the person holding the Ring in trust is of Val Con's own generation.

No wonder the kids are a little tense.

That's some very plain speaking, indeed, between the brothers, and Val Con's assertion that he *can't* marry, which is, by extension, a declaration that he cannot [at this time] give the clan his heir—which really would be the rational thing to do, not only given the dangers inherent in being a Scout, but the other thing Shan isn't saying, which is that—as thin as Korval suddenly has become, and yos'Phelium down to a single pilot—Val Con may well wish to give the clan several children.

Going in, our conceit was that True Lifemates—those pared in what is sometimes called a "wizard's match"—called to each other. That conceit is woven into the fabric of the universe, though the notion that this has been in part engineered by Korval's Damned Meddling Tree has also been woven in. I don't believe that Steve and I had definitively decided on the physical reality of the Tree at the time that *Shan and Priscilla Ride Again* was being written;

certainly, we hadn't formed any strong notion that it was sentient and actively working for its own best interests.

Interesting that only Petrella got to keep her name. I'm guessing that, when the twins were needed again—for *Local Custom*—Petrella and Sella just struck me as too cutesy.

Sharon Lee
June 27, 2015

Chapter the Eleventh

Port Solcintra
Liad

The day was cool with a blur of cloud on the horizon. Come evening, it would rain; one of Liad's warm, gentle deluges; and tomorrow morning would most likely dawn bright and clear.

"Even the weather's funny, Priscilla," Gordy had confided just yesterday. "When it rains, people don't pay any attention at all, an' after a while the sun comes out and dries them off." He'd sighed. "Sure different from home."

Priscilla signed now, remembering her own home and its wild, often dangerous weather. Something for a weatherworker to get her hands into. Here. . .She glanced up at the greenish sky, questions. . .*Nothing there, Goddess. Might as well try for lightning out of stones.*

Which, now that she thought on it, had certain possibilities. Anthora had a way of persuading molecules to vibrate that expended much less of the Witch's energy than she herself had learned in Circle. With that technique, it might indeed be possible to coax a spark or two from a rock.

The idea had appeal. Considering it, Priscilla went with the flow of traffic down the Street of Spices and into the main thoroughfare. She came to herself just opposite Jaernald'a Street and cut across the crowd. Shan and Gordy were to meet her at

Jaernald'a and Paath. They would go to dinner and shuttle up to the *Passage*—

"Your very pardon!"

She started and found herself staring down into a pair of annoyed reddish eyes set in a face that looked—that surely was—

"Fin Ton!"

The eyes blinked. Widened.

"Priss-ella?"

"Of course! Have I changed so much?" She put her hand on his sleeve, laughing.

His smile was a shade uncertain.

"Your accent is much improved. . ."

A woman carrying a pyramid of boxes barely missed walking over him; kept her balance by luck and expert swearing while a man in a Port official's uniform pushed by, audibly muttering about the blockage in traffic.

Priscilla caught Fin Ton's arm and pulled him with her to the mouth of Jaernald'a Street.

"My friend, it's good to see you."

"And good to see you," he acknowledged, speaking the High Tongue in the mode between co-workers. "But how do you come to Solcintra?"

"By ship." She chuckled. "I serve on the *Dutiful Passage*."

"So?" Interest quickened in the expressive face. "Has the redoubtable yo'Lanna then breathed his last? I'd not heard even a whisper."

"Ken Rik? Oh, no—Ken Rik's very much alive! And as evil-tongued as ever."

"It joys me to hear it," said Fin Ton gravely. "So you are not cargo master? You assist, perhaps, the yo'Lanna? He is one who could teach you much of the craft, evil-tongued as he may be."

"True," Priscilla agreed. "But I don't serve in the holds. I'm first mate."

Fin Ton stared; cleared his throat.

"We speak of the same ship? Korval's *Dutiful Passage*?"

"Korval's *Dutiful Passage*," she said firmly.

He drew a deep breath and sighed it out.

"You have risen rapidly. *Ge'shada*." He paused. "One wonders what may have become of Kayzin Ne'Zame."

"She had given her notice before the last trip commenced," Priscilla explained. "It came about that she left ship early, to command *Daxflan*. . ."

"Ah! Now of that, I have heard! But I confess to you, Priss-ella, I thought it no more than a three-glass rumor and paid little heed. Is it truth, then, that Plemia is set back in Balance and Trader Olanek mad?" He touched her sleeve. "It seems now that I had also heard mention of a Terran thodelm involved in the Balance. Yourself, I am certain. Eh? Fortune kisses your cheek."

"The Goddess has been good," she murmured. "But I am reminded: Fin Ton, *you* are owed Balance!"

"*I*?" His face was a study in astonishment. "Surely you mistake—"

"I do not mistake! Did you offer to trade me language lessons for games of GO?"

"So I did—and paid in full!"

"Paid in full," she repeated, black eyes glinting. "You teach me the form, but neglect to explain the circumstance! Is this paid in full?"

"In what instance?" His brow was wrinkled; hands tucked in his belt.

"Oh, only in one instance. I think."

She stepped back and swept the bow between intimates, singing out with perfect intonation, "Fin Ton, I am all joy to see you."

Shock lanced through him. He looked sharply down the street; mercifully saw no one he knew. Priscilla was grinning hugely.

Fin Ton cleared his throat, wondering—

"Good afternoon, Priscilla."

He jerked in a half-turn; stood staring up at the silver-haired giant. His dress was deceptively plain and the great carved amethyst of a master trader gleamed on his big right hand.

"Shan."

Priscilla smiled with joy as she reached along the inner pathways—and encountered the cool slippery mirror of his defenses, shutting her away from him.

Her smile felt stiff on her face, and the day was abruptly cold. She bowed slightly.

"Here is my friend, Fin Ton sig'Kena, Astrogator on *Selda*. Fin Ton, here is Shan yos'Galan..."

Hardly a proper introduction, but neither man seemed to notice. Eyes stretched to their widest, Fin Ton bowed profoundly.

"Master Trader."

Cold silver eyes considered. him. The regal head bent slightly.

"Sir."

"Fin Ton," Priscilla tried breathlessly. "How long are you in port?"

"Several relumma. *Selda* undergoes repairs. Yourself? May I call on you?"

She laughed slightly.

"I would like nothing better, but the *Passage* leaves Solcintra tomorrow and we'll be shuttling up tonight."

"Poor timing," he said ruefully.

"Look for me the next time you're home," she invited. "I'm on Pelthraza Street."

"I will do so," he promised. "But now—I regret. An engagement for which I am very nearly late." He bowed. "Master Trader. I am honored to have met you."

"Sir. Fair fortune to you." Ice cold, the lovely voice.

Fin Ton bowed once more and escaped.

Priscilla glanced at Shan; his defenses were still in place.

"Fin Ton taught me my first Liaden words, when we were on *Selda* together."

"I see," he said unencouragingly.

She changed the subject.

"Where's Gordy?"

"With Val Con. They and Nova and Anthora are all to meet us at Ongit's five minutes ago. I suggest we hurry."

With no further discussion, he turned and started back down Jaernald'a Street.

Priscilla stretched her legs to catch up and went silent beside him all the way to the restaurant.

Auctorial Reflections

OK, I'M NOT HAPPY WITH this chapter *at all*—and not just because of the inexcusably clumsy head-hopping that's going on in it.

First, Priscilla is taking her Balance *far* too lightheartedly. It's as if she knows, intellectually, that Balance is serious, but she still can't resist gently pulling the leg of someone she considers to be a friend. Which is to say, she *hasn't* internalized the fact that, to a Liaden, the intimacies of friendship rank far, far below the necessity to maintain Balance in all things.

Secondly—*really*, Shan? If you weren't a Healer, I'd be embarrassed for you. Since you *are* a Healer, though, I'm wondering what in ghod's name you're on about. You can See perfectly well that Priscilla is having fun with someone she values no more highly than a friend, while the friend's regard for herself is. . .rather cooler. You might be. . .dismayed by the dangerous game she's playing, all in innocence, but *jealous*? And I'm not even going to mention that, the last time you heard that particular phrase, you were delighted at the confusion into which it cast your enemy.

Nope, if I were going on with the project at this point, this chapter would be recast into something useful to the story, and illuminating of the cultural differences. After all, they're going to be going up to the *Passage*, where Priscilla is first mate among a mixed Liaden/Terran crew. This seeming tendency to make light of culture is just the sort of thing that could get her into big trouble on her job.

Sharon Lee
July 4, 2015

Chapter the Twelfth

Port Solcintra

Liad

"Ongit's Galactic Kitchen?"

Priscilla read the Trade words aloud in accents of clear disbelief.

Shan paused, expression approaching amusement.

"You disapprove?"

She waved a hand at the elegant facade encompassing the words.

"I think it's a little misleading."

"And so eminently Liaden. Which is also misleading, by the way. Ongit's is owned by Jackie Ongit, and her husbands and co-wives—Terrans, every one. No, I'm wrong. My ghastly memory. Husband Number Four is Liaden. And the origins of Wife Number Three are in question. But not to her, please. Or to Jackie?"

"Do I need lessons in courtesy?"

A pause before he bowed.

"Of course not, Priscilla. Forgive me."

"Shan. . ."

She caught his arm, eyes searching his face; inner touch sliding off the mirror of his armor.

"At least tell me how I've made you angry."

His hand covered hers briefly.

"I'm not. . .angry. . .my friend. You did nothing but what you must, given circumstance. It's only that I—of course you have lovers, Priscilla. I'm being churlish, which is neither your concern nor your fault. But I do feel the need of privacy."

"Lovers? *Fin Ton*? Shan, that's—"

"Priscilla! Shan!"

She chopped off, eyes going over his shoulder. Gordy and Val Con were bearing down upon them, the boy carrying a large mint-colored shopping bag. He looked frazzled and damp and jubilant as he turned to his escort.

"See? We're not late!"

"Indeed we are," Val Con replied. "It is merely that we are *all* late. My sisters will scold us unmercifully."

"Not Cousin Nova!" Gordy objected, in defense of that glamorous lady.

"Especially Cousin Nova," her foster-brother said without malice. "She has a tongue like a wasp and a great belief that we should all of us behave properly."

"Don't let him frighten you, Gordy," Shan said comfortingly. "By the time Nova's done with me and with Val Con, she might not have much left to say to you and Priscilla. She does so dislike repeating herself. Isn't that so, Brother?"

"Demonstrably," Val Con said, straight-faced.

Shan grinned at him.

"Now, children—Gordon, what's wrong with your hand, please?"

"Nothing! Oh. . ."

Gordy held up his right hand with a proud grin. Priscilla stared and swallowed, averting her eyes. Beside her, Shan sighed.

"Well, let's see: red, green, blue, yellow. Don't tell me you couldn't find rings in additional colors, as well?"

"They had purple," Gordy confessed, smiling fondly at his new possessions. "But I'm going to have a *real* purple ring—like yours."

Shan glanced from the boy's gaudy hand to his own, where the single gem glittered, sullen in the lowering sunlight. Looked up to find Val Con's eyes on him; and sighed again.

"You do know, don't you, Gordy, that very few traders become masters?"

"Yes," said Gordy, unconcerned. "I know."

"You do. In that case, I suggest we go in and face my sisters, children. The sooner the scold is over, the sooner we may eat."

THEY WERE GREETED IN the comfortably appointed entrance room by a dapper Liaden gentleman dressed in the tunic and trousers of the host. He bowed greeting and volunteered the information that Korval-*pernardi* and her sister had just been shown to their room.

"Our last hope dashed," Val Con murmured to Priscilla, who bit her lip.

"Their host (Husband Number Four? Priscilla wondered) politely inquired whether he might not keep the young lord's parcel for him. Gordy declined in tolerable High Liaden, and they were invited to accompany the host a step down the hall.

It was rather more than a step down a deep-carpeted passage lined with doors made elegant with enamel-work. Most were closed, but a few were open, revealing a dazzle of crystal, china, wood and silk. The walls were cream-colored and unadorned; the seating oriented so that each diner had unobstructed view of the room's centerpiece: a holographic 'window.'

Priscilla glimpsed snow-topped peaks, a tumbling river, and a crowded city street, as she went by on Val Con's arm.

"Not too bad, are they?" he murmured for her ears alone. He touched a closed door as they passed it. "This one's very nice. Sol System in Renteld Sector, as seen from Habitat Johnglenn."

"Terra," Priscilla said; and Val Con nodded. "You must come here frequently."

"I believe Anthora comes regularly," he said after a moment. "In the old days. . .This was our mother's favorite restaurant. She loved the Port—the different languages, you know. Mrs. Ongit was a great friend of hers." He smiled. "I must have eaten in every room here, as a child."

Ahead of them, their host paused, opened a door worked in silver, black, and azure; bowed them in.

"There they are!" Anthora cried merrily, while a thunderstorm raged in the center of the room. "Priscilla, my brothers are a bad influence on you!"

Priscilla grinned.

"I'm to blame this time. I saw an old friend in the Port and stopped to talk."

"Much joy, ladies and lords. The meal will shortly begin."

Their host bowed and exited quietly, closing the door behind him.

"Not a moment too soon," commented Shan, waving Priscilla to a chair by Anthora.

"If you had been here timely," Nova observed, "the meal would have begun sooner."

"Would it? I wonder why."

"Cause and effect," Val Con explained softly, sitting at Nova's right hand smiling at her. "I've read a monograph or two on the subject, Brother. The hypothesis is fascinating."

"It sounds bizarre," Shan said, placing Gordy on Nova's other hand and sitting by Priscilla. "Would you do the kindness of lending me the pamphlets, Brother? One must keep abreast of these faddish theories. Especially when one will be going from port to port and exchanging views with all sorts of odd persons. . .Wine, Priscilla? There seems to be rather a quantity by my younger sister's hand, if she'll bestir herself to recall the few manners she has. And while you're pouring for Priscilla, Annie, my love, I find myself in the unusual position of having no glass. Val Con I see is in a similar strait, as is Gordy."

"I'd like water, please," Gordy said.

Shan stared at him in disbelief.

"Water? Whatever for? You're not going to bathe, are you, Gordy?"

"I'm thirsty."

"And you're going to drink water? How peculiar."

"Shan, don't tease him."

Nova poured from the pitcher at her place; and handed the boy a brimming crystal mug. "Ice cold, Cousin. Pray tell me if you would like more."

Gordy received the glass reverently from her slim hand.

"Thank you. . ."

"Always of service."

She turned her violet eyes to her eldest brother.

"Jackie visited earlier. She was sorry not to see you. Her schedule does not permit another visit this evening."

"I'm sorry to have missed her, as well. Jackie would make you joyful, Priscilla," Shan said, handing a glass down-table. "Your wine approaches, Brother. Be of good heart. Gordy, please don't think I'm prying, but what is in that parcel? It would have been quite safe with Mr. Ongit the Fourth, you know. He's rather particular in his care of other people's property."

Gordy glanced at Val Con, who nodded slightly.

"I—ummm—bought some things and I wanted to give them to—to everybody at once. To say thank you for—for fostering me and for—caring—about what happens and stuff. . ."

His voice faded abruptly and he dove into the bag.

"This is for Anthora," he said, pushing a shallow box wrapped in pale pink into Shan's hands. Wordlessly, he passed it down.

Anthora smiled prettily.

"Thank you, Gordy."

She tugged at the ribbon, lifted the top—and laughed.

"Well done, Cousin! The very thing to tame this mop of mine!"

She held up a red wooden comb carved in a rich profusion of birds and flowers, then caught up a handful of unruly dark hair, twisted in sharply and pinned it in place. The red wood shone like a coronation gem.

"So!"

"It looks pretty," said Gordy, unself-consciously.

"So it does, sister," Nova added. "You chose very well, Cousin."

He vanished into his bag again and held out a slimmer packet.

"This one's for you."

"My thanks."

She unwrapped it neatly; smiled with rare fullness.

"'The Poetry of Samuel Delaney,'" she read aloud. She bent over and kissed the young cheek.

"Well done, Gordy."

He gulped and pulled out a heftier package.

"Shan."

Yiptarean brandy, stasis-sealed at the moment of its perfection. Easily a cantra the bottle. Shan set the gift carefully before him; glanced over Gordy's head to Val Con, who was staring into the thunderstorm.

"Thank you, my child," he said to Gordy. "The gift is pleasing." He paused. "You don't have to give gifts to thank us, Gordy. We appreciate them, but we *wanted* you to be with us."

"I know," Gordy said, just as quietly. "But I wanted to give you all gifts—I'm so happy to be here. . ." He looked in danger of snuffling; snapped his fingers with shocking suddenness. "Crelm! What a dope!"

Back he went into the bag.

"Priscilla—I hope you like 'em."

A small box enveloped in the crimson silk of a jeweler. The earrings within were silver chains, matched black diamonds handing at the end of each.

"Gordy. . .Thank you, dear. They're lovely."

"You're welcome. . ."

Gordy stood and reached into the bag once more.

"Val Con," he said.

Both eyebrows lifted.

"Not, surely, Val Con."

Gordy grinned.

"Fooled you! They wouldn't wrap it, though." He bent over and put a small, gleaming something on the cloth before the man.

"Ah."

A sound of surprised pleasure. Val Con picked the object up, twisted—and was suddenly holding a slim and businesslike dirk.

"My very thanks to you, brother's-son."

He glanced up with a grin. "To speak with the sarl merchant, indeed!"

Gordy laughed.

And the door opened to admit the beginning of the meal.

Auctorial Reflections

I SEE WE HAD SOME SENTENCE fragments left at the bottom of the box. Too bad about that.

That's nice that Gordy gave Nova a volume of Chip's poems. I hadn't recalled that she was poetical, but she seems genuinely pleased, as well she might be.

Is it just me, or are people forever giving Anthora combs? In *I Dare* she'd been wearing the comb Daav had carved for Aelliana in *Scout's Progress*—and *that's* interesting because it seems to me that this comb and Aelliana's are very similar in design–which didn't seem up to "taming" her "mop," at all.

I'm a little displeased with that bottle of brandy for Shan, though we have Andre Norton to thank for its cellar. But, really, bottles of brandy are like aftershave; the sort of gift you give an uncle you don't know very well. I feel Gordy could have done better, with a little thought. Certainly, *Val Con* ought to have done better.

It was clever of Gordy to fool Val Con, even if–just maybe—Val Con let him.

If I were doing it now, I might have had black tourmalines on Priscilla's earrings; because Maine has taught me that black tourmalines are "worthless," whereas black diamonds at least *sound* spendy. On the other hand, I might have let it go, simply because more people understand "diamond" than "tourmaline."

Also, this whole chapter wants a stern going-over with a red pen, with a special eye toward the tone of the whole scene–but that's the nature of first drafts.

So, that.

Now. What I really want to talk about is Ongit's Galactic Kitchen.

Ongit's is one of those places in the Liaden Universe® that bear much more weight for the authors than for readers. Steve and I know Ongit's inside and out; we've been there for lunch, and dinner—and for breakfast with Jackie, at the back bar, because Ongit's doesn't serve breakfast. We've hosted a number of parties there, and observed at least two Dangerous Assignations, yet. . .

Ongit's appears in *Mouse and Dragon*—as neutral ground, which it is, ohmyyes. Jackie worked hard to ensure that her place of business was neutral territory. She had to do some unsavory things, back when she was just getting set up—only herself and Mr. Ongit the First, before even the wooing of their first co-wife—in order to make her point, and to impress upon High Port, Mid Port, and Low Port that she was serious *and* competent. The point did stick, and nowadays Jackie might be able to rest on her reputation. Or not.

Ongit's also appears in "Certain Symmetry," as the place where Pat Rin and Luken meet for dinner; and in this fragment, never published.

. . .not much air time for a venue that the authors know so well.

And this, Gentle Readers, is part of How We Do It. The worldbuilding part, where people say—"But your world is so real! How do you do it?"

This is how we do it. There are places, and people, that we've dealt with intimately, sometimes over a period of years. Such places, imaginary as they may be. . .accrete believability. I know this, as I know few things in life—*Ongit's exists*. I've *been* there. And let me tell you, Wife Number Three is a terrible flirt.

This capacity for self-delusion and absolute belief in the existence of imaginary people and places, is also what allowed Theo to leap onto the page as a fully realized person at the end of *I Dare*. Steve and I had known—and known about—Theo for years—maybe a decade—before Stephe Pagel asked us to write an epilogue, so that people wouldn't think that there would be no more Liaden adventures.

Sharon Lee
July 10, 2015

Chapter the Thirteenth

Dutiful Passage
Liad Orbit
12.00 Hours

T he shuttle lodged firmly and the magnetics died as the man in back reached for the release. He was on his feet before the pilot's laconic Trade instructed that all might now leave by the rear door.

Touching his belt to make certain that the all-important papers still rode secure, the man did just that.

He stopped in the center of the reception area, craning like any tourist, while his former shuttle-mates flowed, talking and laughing, around him.

On *that* wall, the venerable Tree-and-Dragon, displayed on every Korval vessel, yet never so prominently as on this, the flagship. On this other wall, a collage of the images of distinguished visitors to the ship. Under one's feet, Bilshedian carpet; above one's head, crystals, cunningly refracting and reflecting the chamber's light.

Before him, a tow-headed child in neat shirt and trousers. The badge on his shoulder read "Arbuthnot."

"Master tel'Domit?"

The man bowed.

The child bowed also, though belatedly, which put the man in forcible mind of his own young heir.

"I'm Gordy Arbuthnot. Cap'n yos'Galan asked me to bring you to him."

"I am honored," he murmured properly, though Trade robbed the words of a measure of their value. A glance at the young face brought forth a glimmer of smile.

"I am happy to go with you to the captain, young sir," he hinted, and the boy laughed.

"Crelm! What a dummy I am!" he said in rueful Terran and gestured widely toward the door. "Right this way."

"COME!" A VOICE CALLED and the door slid away before them. The boy led the way into the room and bowed before the untidy desk.

"Cap'n yos'Galan, here is Master tel'Domit, come to see you."

"Is he? How delightful of him to visit, don't you think so, Priscilla?"

"Yes, Captain."

The man behind the desk was white-haired, silver eyed and big-nosed, built to Terran specifications, rather than Liaden. None of this surprised.

What *did* surprise was the woman who stood nearby. His moment of incredulous observation yielded the information that she was astonishingly lovely; and then he must need bow and pull the treasured papers from their safe-place and murmur all that was correct.

"Mich tel'Domit, Master Pilot, and third in command of *Sunjumper*, come to take position as second mate of *Dutiful Passage*, if Captain yos'Galan is willing."

"Willing? Why shouldn't I be willing? The question is, sir, if you are willing. I've known persons of quite strong character to beg leave to quit the ship after being met by Gordy. If you find you simply can't bear it, tell me, and no dishonor will attach to you."

Mich straightened slowly, buying time to sort out the spate of Terran words. A quick glance at the boy showed that he was grinning.

So.

"The young sir was most helpful," he managed in the cumbersome Terran tongue. "I report to the captain in joy."

Silver eyes regarded him blandly.

"How many Terrans were on *Sunjumper's* roster?"

"At the time I leave my post, there are—were—no Terrans in the crew. When first I come, there are two." He frowned with the effort to clarify. "They go to other Korval ships, sir. Promoted."

"I see."

A wave of a big hand, Master Trader's ring glinting.

"My dreadful manners! Priscilla, here is Mich tel'Domit, who will be second mate. Master tel'Domit, this is Priscilla Delacroix y Mendoza, First Mate."

"I am pleased to meet you, Mich tel'Domit," the woman said in welcome High Liaden.

He faced her and bowed with relief.

"I am pleased to meet you, Priscilla Dela Croyee—" He floundered and straightened, hot-faced. "Forgive me."

She laughed softly.

"Priscilla Mendoza is perfectly adequate."

Astonishingly lovely, and barely more than a halfling, now that he saw her fully. No need to look far for the reason she held so exalted a post. . . He bowed once more.

"Priscilla Mendoza."

"Very good."

Captain yos'Galan came around the desk and held out his hand. Mich handed him the papers. The slanted silver brows rose.

"I meant to shake your hand."

He bowed then, with a flourish of welcome.

"I am pleased you are here, Mich tel'Domit," he said, the High Tongue pure as crystal chime. "May the luck send that we all work well, to mutual profit."

He turned to the woman, the first mate, slipping effortlessly back into Terran.

"All right, Priscilla; he's all yours."

THEY WERE WALKING SIDE-by-side down Corridor Axis Teluf-Vange, having passed the Library and heading toward crew quarters. Mich had learned that this was his superior's second trip upon *Dutiful Passage*, where she had previously held the rank of Pet Librarian. She claimed to be a first class pilot, and that he did not doubt, though she was, perhaps, young for the rank. He had also learned other things that called into question his first guess at her abilities, though not her primary function. It was known that Korval valued competence. Even, one assumed, in a pleasure-love.

They rounded a corner, silent for the nonce, and into the middle of an altercation.

"I do not care," the small woman was saying with passion, "if it is what everyone else on your homeworld does! It is perfectly dreadful, Rah Stee, and I hope you will not persist in it!"

"I like it," the man, obviously Terran, said mildly. He fingered the brush of hair between nose and mouth nervously.

"Think it adds dash. Give it a chance and I bet you'll like it, too. Anyhow, it's my face, not—Cilla!"

"It is *certainly* not Priscilla," agreed the woman, but her companion had lumbered forward, flinging his arms wide in a clumsy hug.

"Hello, Rusty."

The first mate suffered herself to be embraced, and raised no objection when the man kissed her cheek. Mich schooled his own face, carefully looking at nothing. It was not inconceivable that the two were kin.

"Nice mustache."

"Oh, no, Priscilla, do not tell him so!"

The Liaden woman flung forward, catching the mate's hand.

"Tell him it is dreadful and that he must make it go away!"

"Lina." The Terran woman's smile was soft. "It's good to see you."

"Ah, and it is good to see you—and we all forget our manners! See, Rah Stee, we have a guest—you must face him with hair on your mouth!"

"Doesn't bother me," the man muttered.

The first mate laughed.

"Mich tel'Domit, Second Mate, here are Lina Faaldom, Librarian and Healer; and Rusty Morgenstern, Chief Radio Tech."

The Liaden woman bowed.

"I am pleased to meet you, Mich tel'Domit."

"Hi," said Rusty Morgenstern.

Mich bowed and chose careful Terran words.

"I am pleased to meet both Librarian and Radio Tech."

Lina Faaldom's honey-brown eyes caught his, and she smiled.

"We are keeping you from your orientation, I think. Pay no mind to us. It is always this way, though not, I think, to the depth of this folly. Priscilla will tell you."

"They fight all the time," the first mate said, laughing her soft, seductive laugh. "I'll see you both later."

"We've completed the circuit," she told Mich as they continued down the hall. "Why don't I leave you at your cabin so you can get yourself sorted out? Then, I'll guide you to Prime in an hour."

It took a moment to understand that the question was in fact an order. Mich bowed hurriedly.

"Of course."

"Fine," said Priscilla, and turned down a side hall.

Auctorial Reflections

NOW, HERE'S SOMEONE with a legitimate *melant'i* concern. Mich tel'Domit is second mate, which means that part of his job is to support the first mate. But if the first mate's previous position on the Passage was pet librarian (which, by the way, it was not), how much can she know about her job? How much is he going to be expected to cover for her, and is he being set up as the goat, in case something goes catastrophically wrong?

Even if Mich had the whole story—Priscilla signed on part-way through the last trip as Pet Librarian, rose to second mate and thence properly to first, filling the gap in command created by Kayzin Ne'Zame's leaving in order to take *Daxflan* home—that's.

. .meteoric. And he's *still* gotta be asking himself how much this woman actually knows about her job.

First mate is a position you typically reach after years of service in increasingly sensitive positions. Which also gives us some idea of how old Mich is—another clue being that Mich sees "a child" when he looks at Gordy and someone who is "barely more" than a halfling when he looks at Priscilla.

On supposes that Shan has chosen Mich as second mate for *a reason,* and not just because he has time in grade. And, certainly, choosing an older, steadier, more experienced officer to support the new first mate isn't a *completely* daft thing to do. Though it might have been nice if he would have Communicated More Fully with the man than he seems to have done.

Unless it's A Test. One isn't always certain, with Shan.

Speaking to Mich, himself. . .Clearly, he needs some time in the sleep learner for his Terran, and he also needs to spend some time with the Cultural Officer (is there specific mention of the Cultural Officer back this far?), brushing up—or becoming acquainted—with Terran manners and mores—deficiencies which incline me more toward A Test, or even Several Tests. That said, his *temperament* seems suited to the *Passage's* peculiar culture. Yes, he's confused by some of the things he's encountered, but he's not *horrified.* A planet-bound Liaden would have fainted dead away by this point. Or challenged the whole crew to a duel.

. . .THINKING ABOUT the story framed thus far, it seems as if Steve and I wanted to talk about assumptions—the assumption that a "little boy" cannot have abilities or interests that baffle his elders; the assumption that people who appear to have been elevated beyond their abilities must have arrived there via Suspicious Avenues.

It's perhaps unfortunate that, as the cast of characters is structured, the person to whom some Very Serious Assumptions have been applied is female—because these are exactly the same sort of assumptions that continue to be made of women today, and are therefore either "invisible," or "feminist"—and in either case dismissible by a certain segment of readers.

Had it been *Peter* Mendoza who had fallen under Shan's care and into his heart, our point would have been sharper*. On the other hand, given that we were writing this in 1986/1988—let's split the difference and call it 28 years ago—*Conflict of Honors* wouldn't have gotten into orbit with Peter and Shan aboard.

---

*Funny how swapping things around in a story sometimes gets people to think. When we were writing *Fledgling/Saltation* and the point came up that established female scholars often took younger men as their *onagrata*, thereby casting aside older male scholars, and leaving them on their own in diminished circumstances, we apparently hit a nerve in some of our male readership.

"That's just not fair!" one young man told me, hotly.

"Oh," I said; "isn't it?"

Sharon Lee
July 13, 2015

Chapter the Fourteenth

Dutiful Passage
Tripday 1
Shipyear 66
20.00 Hours
Outbound of Liaden Space

P riscilla rounded the corner into the Captain's Hall, sighing. Orbit had been broken smoothly and even now the *Passage* progressed toward the Jump-point, pliant under Vilobar's experienced hands. Third Mate Gil Don Balatrin had the bridge-watch now, and would keep it until the moment of Jump, when he would return it to the captain and first mate.

The red-striped door appeared; she lay her hand against the annunciator. Without hesitation, the panel slid away before her: First Mate's Privilege.

"Good evening, Priscilla!"

Voice gay, pattern showing hard edged joy, coupled with a tang of wild relief.

"Escaped at last—and not a moment too soon! Another day on that planet's surface and I would have presented myself to the Healers as severely impaired."

"Not as bad as that, surely?"

He glanced up from an unruly printout strip, blunt fingers still tapping and straightening.

"At least as bad as that. Liadens do pale quickly, don't you find?"

She perched on the arm of a visitor's chair; expanded her attention slightly, so that she read nuance; tasted intensity.

"You're Liaden," she pointed out. "I don't find that you've paled at all."

He laughed and flung up a brown hand.

"Nor will, I wager! Will you drink, Priscilla? I'll just get this together and join you at the sofa. I've seen enough of this desk today—and for days to come! Or at least until next on-shift. I'd appreciate a glass of the red, if you're inclined to bring it."

"Certainly."

She went quietly to the bar, pouring a glass of white and one of red while papers continued to rustle at her back. Shan was a creature of bright delights and warm joys, each emotion sharply realized. Part of that was training, of course. An empath who cannot control her own emotions is hardly able to use her gift as the Goddess intended, for the succor of others.

But much of it was Shan himself, and the frenzied, cutting static was as much unlike him as lightless depression.

"Well," he said behind her, "I think there's finally an end to it! You wouldn't think an individual of Mr. dea'Gauss' personal reticence would be quite so voluble on-screen, would you?"

She picked up the glasses and took them to the comfortable cluster of sofa, table and chair.

"Do you have something from Mr. dea'Gauss already? We just left orbit!"

He dropped into the chair and took the glass of red from her.

"Thank you, my friend. Mr. dea'Gauss is constrained neither by time, nor by distance, nor by orbit. Godlike, he has reached out and deposited—what is the damn' thing called, anyway? Aha!

Cross-Linear Agreement of Fostering Between Line yos'Galan and Line Mendoza in the Instance of Gordon Finn Arbuthnot, Line Davis."

He reverently placed the pile of printout on the table before her.

"I've taken the liberty of providing you with a hardcopy file for your Line's records."

She picked the papers up and riffled them. Twenty-one finely printed pages.

"This is seven pages longer than the lease I signed on my house."

"Leasing a child is rather more complex than leasing a house, you know, Priscilla."

She laughed.

"I suppose. Well, I'll read it later, and—"

Shan cleared his throat.

"Forgive me, Priscilla. Mr. dea'Gauss requires a beamed confirmation from you before the *Passage* leaves Liaden space. Signed hardcopy verification may be sent by courier from our next port."

"Before—He could have gotten this to me any time during the past month! Why wait until now, when it's an imposition and a—"

"Mr. dea'Gauss gives me to understand that the unusual nature of the document caused much initial delay among Liaden contract-binders. Normally, you see, Nova would have been named as Gordy's foster-mother, since the foster-father has not lifemated. However, since Katy-Rose expressed her preference that you stand as mother to her son. . ."

He raised his glass.

"There is a summary at the beginning. Two pages of Terran. I believe it to be an accurate representation of the document. And you can include any quibbles, questions or changes with the courier packet."

She riffled the pages again; found the summer tucked between pages one and two of the actual document and began to read. The print was even finer than that of the contract, and Mr. dea'Gauss' Terran ran to rolling periods, but she set the pages aside within five minutes and picked up her own glass.

"It does seem like a lot of effort," she commented. "I've said I'll stand as mother to Gordy. What do my heirs and assignees have to do with it? Why would my 'estate' want to hold Gordy, should I return to the Goddess? What—"

"Liadens," Shan broke in gently, "dearly love contracts, Priscilla. Consider how much easier it is to be honorable when all conditions and terms are spelled out and known by everyone ahead of time. Ambiguity leads to dispute. *I* don't think you—or your estate!—plans anything nefarious regarding Gordy. Likely Mr. dea'Gauss doesn't think so, either, but you can never be sure; the man has a devious mind. Better to have the contract filed and at hand as a reference. Then everyone can be easy. Especially people who have no tolerance for the unusual. Which brings us back to the vast majority of Liadens."

"Which in turn brings up the subject of the second mate."

She sat forward, glass cradled in long ivory fingers.

"Shan, I barely understand *my* duties! How can I train a second mate?"

He blinked.

"I suppose you will have to learn together, Priscilla. Good way to cement a positive working relationship. The man's excellent, by the way. You reviewed his record?"

"Yes. He worked his way from apprentice pilot and junior mechanic into the command structure—almost as unusual as a promotion from pet librarian to first mate. . ."

She hesitated.

"I saw something else."

"Yes? A propensity for snakes, perhaps? Send him to Ken Rik."

She frowned into her glass.

"We met Rusty and Lina. Rusty hugged me and kissed my cheek, and the spike of shock I got from Mich—you'd have thought Rusty had struck me, Shan!"

Whiff of metal; glimpse of green, both quickly shielded.

"He *is* Liaden, Priscilla. That sort of thing's bound to be a shock to him. If you find he's less than flexible—but it's your decision. Were the captain's advice solicited, I'd suggest giving him some time to find his feet and re-evaluate around mid-trip."

She nodded and sipped, scanning as closely as she dared. The static had increased measurably. Of jealously, she could find no trace.

"Might I use your console?" she asked, rising. "I'll just send my affirmation to Mr. dea'Gauss now."

Auctorial Reflections

I *knew* it was a Test!

fist pump

Ahem. OK, leaving aside the objection that the captain and the first mate should have had this conversation Some Time Back, and that the first mate ought to have been involved in the hiring of the second mate. . .

No, wait. . .

Yes. I can actually sort-of handwave that away. Let's see. . .

In *Plan B*, Ren Zel tells us that, in the absence of a first mate (for instance, in a situation where the first mate must rise to captain), second mate rises to first; third to second; and the captain names a new third mate from among the qualified crew. I believe (though I cannot at the moment prove) that Gil Don Balatrin, the third mate, refused the promotion to second when it was offered to him in *Conflict of Honors*, on the grounds that he was not fit for the duty.

Now! Kayzin Ne'Zame was leaving the ship at the end of the last voyage, anyway, and Janice—Janice?—would have been expected to rise to first, since she had time in grade on the *Passage,* and was known to the crew—except Janice screwed up and Shan appointed Priscilla second mate, with instructions to Kayzin to groom her for first. This set of circumstances leaves the position of second mate open, and Shan—possibly with *Kayzin's* input; in fact, he'd be crazy not to seek Kayzin's advice, given how many years she had served the *Passage*—hires Mich.

None of this explains why Shan didn't talk Mich over with Priscilla, *too*, but at least they're talking now.

Speaking of a day late and a cantra short, Mr. dea'Gauss is being something of a nuisance. As things have shaken out in the Universe over the intervening years, the *qe'andra* both write and underwrite contracts, as well as serving as accountants—one has the notion that they account both financial matters and matters of Balance. In *Mouse and Dragon*, we see that Mr. dea'Gauss' firm is quite large. Surely such an enterprise would have an underwriter on-staff. Of course, *Mouse and Dragon* was written many, many years after this fragment staring Shan and Priscilla, and I doubt we'd given much thought to the details of Mr. dea'Gauss' vocation, or the size-and-shape of the business itself.

This is the penultimate chapter of this novel fragment. Next week, we'll conclude our business here.

Sharon Lee
July 24, 2015

Chapter the Fifteenth

The *Passage*, the Town, and the Tradebar

T he pool was deserted, Mich thought, as his first glance cataloged the area. He had dropped his coverup and was heading for the diving board before he saw his error.

Standing bent slightly forward on the edge of the pool, face showing an intensity of concentration worthy of the most knotty piloting proble, was the cabin boy, Gordy Arbuthnot.

Mich broke stride, watching quietly as the boy deliberately filled his lungs, brought his arms back, forward—and dove.

There was no showiness about it, nor even much grace, except that it failed of being a bellyflop; merely a dogged, businesslike entering of the pool, perfectly adequate of its type, and surely nothing to warrant such concentration?

Even as he thought so, the boy's head broke water and he struck out without haste nor hesitation for the further side. Touching the wall, he executed a smooth roll and was on his way back. Mich came forward and sat crosslegged on the edge, awaiting his arrival.

Gordy touched the wall; looked up with a girn on his wet face and began to tread water.

"Hi."

"Good shift, young sir," Mich replied in his slowly-improving Terran. "It is a fine time for a swim, when one first leaves duty."

"I guess," the boy said doubtfully. "I like to get it over with first thing, though. Makes everything else that happens during the day easy—even one of Ken Rik's tongue-lashings."

He paused, and evidently sober thought led him to a qualification.

"Well, nothing'll make one of Ken Rik's scolds *easy*. . ."

By this time somewhat acquainted with the cargo master's powers of discourse, Mich smiled.

"I understand. But do I hear that the young sir does not enjoy the swim?"

"It's not so bad," Gordy said, though without much conviction. "The reason I do it, thought, is because Val Con made me promise I would swim every day—at least four laps."

"Val Con?" Mich frowned, then inclined his head in recognition. "Nadelm Korval, this will be."

"Yeah. . ." But there was more. "Priscilla says that four laps is OK at first, but once that starts to get easy, I should add another one, to make it a challenge again."

He sighed.

"The first mate is wise," Mich murmured.

"Sure she is, that's why she's first mate," Gordy said. "But she was telling me as my foster-mother, see, so that makes it even worse."

"Worse?" wondered Mich, controlling twitching lips with an effort.

"Worse," Gordy confirmed gloomily.

"'cause four laps is starting to be a piece of cake, so I'm going to *have* to make it five. And pretty soon, five'll be easy, so I'll have to do to *six*. . ."

He glared at Mich, who held up his hands, showing them empty of threat.

"Val Con's idea of a joke," the boy finished, darkly.

"No doubt," Mich returned, politely. "But, if the young sir would explain another point—I had understood that Shan yos'Galan speaks as your father."

"He does," said the boy matter-of-factly; "and Priscilla speaks as my mother. Mr. dea'Gauss drew up a contract, and everything."

He glanced at his wrist and then back to Mich.

"I don't want to be rude, but I've got to do some more laps and it's getting late. . ."

Mich waved a dismissing hand.

"Pray do not wait upon me, sir."

He watched the boy finish his laps, struggling with the implications. A joint fostering? And they two certainly lovers, but never lifemates. It was mad—against all tradition and sense. How could the child's education be soundly charted, with the necessities of two clans to heed? How if pleasure ended and *nubiat'a* given? Did the giver of the parting-gift take charge of the child, or the recipient?

Mich sighed in frustrated disapproval. Well and good to say that the dea'Gauss had written the contract—certainly no lesser could aspire to meet the task—but these were matters heavy with tradition—

His thoughts were interrupted by the splash of Gordy Arbuthnot coming out of the pool. He rose and bowed, received a bow in return, and watched the boy out of the pool-room.

Then, he strode down to the diving board, bounced twice and launched into a smooth arc, slicing the water like a knife.

Auctorial Reflections

CLEARLY, THIS IS NOT a complete chapter, though the title apparently thought it was going to be going places and doing things, and yet. . .this is the last we have. Gordy beginning his work shift, Mich ending his.

The business with the fostering shakes out some interesting details from Mich's viewpoint as a Liaden, but—it's in the wrong place, if he's been aboard and working long enough to have become acquainted with Ken Rik in a Snit. Though I suppose that could have happened during their first meeting, Ken Rik being Ken Rik.

MANY TIMES DURING THE unfolding of this fragment of a novel, people have asked that we "finish" it.

At this point, that's really not very likely.

Not just because the plot doesn't know where the heck it's going, or that Shan's working on my last nerve—well, that's part of it, but not, maybe, for the reason you think—or even that the writing's. . .a trifle gaumy* here and there.

We did, after all, have some idea of where we thought the story would be going, even if it's a little bit of a puzzle how all the various pieces are going to snap together. That's just what writing fiction is—building the pieces of the jigsaw puzzle before you know, exactly, what the finished picture will look like.

Back in 1986/88, for instance, we thought that (part of) this story would have to do with Priscilla becoming reconciled with her mother, whom she encounters when the *Passage* stops at the Galaxy's Biggest Textile Market in order to do some shopping. A run-in, large or small, with the Juntavas, has clearly been called for in the material we've have before us, though whether Anmary

Mendoza was dealing Gray, or was caught by chance in a Juntavas Manuever I don't know, now—and likely didn't know then, either.

And it remains a mystery, how Gordy's swimming lessons figure into it all. No, wait! I've got an idea about that. . .

But, anyway, it's not the fact that the 18,586 words of fiction we've just read are. . .inconclusive, or even the fact that there are 80,000ish words yet to write, or that we have books before it under contract.

The reason we probably won't be writing *this book* is: Time

A decade has passed in-Universe between the end of *Conflict of Honors* and the beginning of *Dragon in Exile.* Shan and Priscilla have been together as a team for every one of those ten years, though they only "officially" became lifemates during *Plan B.* (There's an argument, in *Carpe Diem*, between Nova and Shan, regarding his desire to lifemate Priscilla, and the necessity of Korval-in-Trust to hold him free for contract marriage, should it come to pass that Val Con is no longer available to the clan.)

While there are things that I regret not having had the opportunity to do—such as building the relationship between Priscilla and Shan's powers, watching them forging their first links to each other, and growing into the team they now are—the existence of *Alliance of Equals* (coming to a bookstore near *you* July-ish 2016, and as an eArc about 3 months prior to that) would make carving that story out properly much more work than fun. We can retcon—we have retconned!—but there's just not enough elbow room, as I'm eying things, to fit an early "discovery" novel for Shan and Priscilla into the space after *Conflict.*

So, now we're at an end of it. Steve and I want to thank all of you for your attention, your comments, your support. It's been fun, and interesting, for us—and we hope for you, too.

*(Maine dialect) also *gaummy, gawmy, gohmey*—clumsy, awkward; "gom" one who is clumsy or awkward. Possibly related to *gorm[less]*.

Sharon Lee
August 1, 2015

ABOUT THE AUTHORS

Maine-based writers Sharon Lee and Steve Miller teamed up in the late 1980s to bring the world the story of Kinzel, an inept wizard with a love of cats, a thirst for justice, and a staff of true power.

Since then, the husband-and-wife team have written dozens of short stories and twenty plus novels, most set in their star-spanning, nationally-bestselling, Liaden Universe®.

Before settling down to the serene and stable life of a science fiction and fantasy writer, Steve was a traveling poet, a rock-band reviewer, reporter, and editor of a string of community newspapers.

Sharon, less adventurous, has been an advertising copywriter, copy editor on night-side news at a small city newspaper, reporter, photographer, and book reviewer.

Both credit their newspaper experiences with teaching them the finer points of collaboration.

Steve and Sharon are jointly the recipients of the E. E. "Doc" Smith Memorial Award for Imaginative Fiction (the Skylark), one of the oldest awards in science fiction. In addition, their work has won the much-coveted Prism Award (*Mouse and Dragon* and *Local Custom*), as well as the Hal Clement Award for Best Young Adult Science Fiction (*Balance of Trade*), and the Year's Best Military and Adventure SF Readers' Choice Award ("Wise Child").

Sharon and Steve passionately believe that reading fiction ought to be fun, and that stories are entertainment.

Steve and Sharon maintain a web presence at: http://korval.com

NOVELS BY SHARON LEE
AND STEVE MILLER

The Liaden Universe®
  Fledgling
Saltation
Mouse and Dragon
Ghost Ship
Dragon Ship
Necessity's Child
Trade Secret
Dragon in Exile
Alliance of Equals
The Gathering Edge
Neogenesis
Accepting the Lance
Trader's Leap
Omnibus Editions
The Dragon Variation
The Agent Gambit
Korval's Game
The Crystal Variation
Story Collections
A Liaden Universe Constellation: Volume 1

A Liaden Universe Constellation: Volume 2
A Liaden Universe Constellation: Volume 3
A Liaden Universe Constellation: Volume 4
The Fey Duology
Duainfey
Longeye
Gem ser'Edreth
The Tomorrow Log

NOVELS BY SHARON LEE

The Carousel Trilogy
Carousel Tides
Carousel Sun
Carousel Seas
Jennifer Pierce Maine Mysteries
Barnburner
Gunshy

THANK YOU

Thank you for your support of our work.
Sharon Lee and Steve Miller

Made in the USA
Coppell, TX
05 July 2021